A Book of Fairy Tale Foxes

SELECTIONS FROM FAVORITE
FOLKLORE STORIES

EDITED BY CLIFTON JOHNSON
ILLUSTRATED BY FRANK A. NANKIVELL

A Book of Fairy Tale Foxes:
Selections from Favorite Folklore Stories
edited by Clifton Johnson
Illustrated by Frank A. Nankivell
Gently re-edited by K. J. Joyner

Published by The Writers of the Apocalypse
117 N Carbon Street, PMB 208
Marion, IL 62959

Find our books online at: http://woksprint.com

ISBN Print: 978-1-944322-67-0
Digital: 978-1-944322-71-7

Cover assembly: K. J. Joyner

A BOOK OF
FAIRY TALE
FOXES

ILLUSTRATED BY

FRANK A. NANKIVELL

TABLE OF CONTENTS

THE ROBBER FOX AND THE LITTLE RED HEN 9

REYNARD'S RIDE 13

THE FOX AND THE WOLF'S DAUGHTER 16

THE SLEEPING FOX AND THE BOY WITH A STONE 21

THE FOX WHO DID NOT WANT TO BE A HEATHEN 24

THE LIMPING FOX 27

HOW MRS. FOX MARRIED AGAIN 35

THE FOX AND THE BOASTFUL ROOSTER 40

REYNARD AND THE FOXHUNTER 44

THE FOX AND THE OLD CAT AND DOG 47

THE TWO FOXES AND THE HOT ROLLS 55

A FOX AND HIS FRIENDS 59

THE HUNGRY FOX AND HIS BREAKFAST 70

REYNARD AND THE LITTLE BIRDS 75

THE FOX AND HIS FIVE HUNGRY COMRADES 78

THE CRAFTY FOX AND THE INDUSTRIOUS GOOSE 91

THE FOX AND THE WICKED WOLF 95

THE FOX WHO BECAME A SHEPHERD 102

THE FOX, THE WOLF, AND THE CHEESE 107

HOW THE CAT OUTWITTED THE FOX 113

THE FOX, THE BEAR, AND THE POOR FARMER
.... 118

THE PROUD FOX AND THE YOUNG PRAIRIE
CHICKEN.. 124

HOW THE FOX AND THE CRAB RAN A RACE
.... 127

THE FOX WITH A SACKFUL OF TRICKS 130

REYNARD AND HIS ADVENTURES 133

THE ROBBER FOX AND THE LITTLE RED HEN

Once UPON A TIME there was a little red hen who lived in a house by herself at the edge of a piece of woodland.

On the other side of the wood dwelt a robber fox with his mother. One morning, right after breakfast, the robber fox said to his mother: "I am going to catch the little red hen today. So make a fire, and get the pot boiling. We'll cook her as soon as I come back and have her for dinner."

Then he slung a bag over his shoulder and started for the little red hen's house.

The little red hen never suspected any danger, and she did her morning work as usual. After a while she looked at the clock to see what time it was. "Well," she said, "now I must begin to get dinner, and the first thing I'll do is to step out into the yard for a few chips to make my fire burn more briskly."

Out she went, but while she was filling her apron

with the chips the robber fox came along and slipped into the house without her seeing him. He hid behind the door, and said, "I'll catch her easily enough, now." Pretty soon the little red hen came in, and she was just going to shut the door when she saw the fox. Then she was so frightened that she dropped all her chips and flew up to a peg in the wall.

"Ha, ha!" the robber fox laughed, "it won't take me long to bring you down from there." And he began running round and round after his tail.

The little red hen kept turning about on the peg to watch him, and in a few minutes she got so dizzy that she fell off.

Immediately the fox picked her up, put her in his bag, and started for home feeling very smart. By and by he grew tired and sat down to rest. The little red hen did not like traveling in a bag, and she did not want to be eaten. She began to wonder if she could plan to escape, and she thought and thought until she happened to think that she had her scissors in her pocket. Without wasting anymore time she took the scissors and snipped a hole in the bag and jumped out.

The ground just there was strewn with stones, and the little red hen picked up several as large as she could lift and put them in the bag in her place. Then she ran home as fast as she could go.

After a time the fox got up and went on. "How heavy this little hen is!" he said to himself. "She must be very plump and fat. Ah, won't she make a good dinner!" And he smacked his lips at the thought of how nice she would taste.

When he came in sight of his house he saw his mother standing in the doorway watching for him, and he called out, "Hi, mother! Have you got the pot boiling?"

"Yes, yes," his mother replied, "and have you got the little red hen?"

"She's here in this bag that I have on my shoulder," was his answer, "and she'll make a fine dinner."

He walked on into the house, and his mother led the way to the fireplace. "Now," he said, "when I count three, you take the cover off the pot, and I'll pop the little red hen right into the hot water."

"Very well," his mother responded.

"All ready," the fox said; "one, two, three!"

His mother took the cover off, and splash went the stones into the boiling water, and the pot tipped over and scalded the robber fox and his mother to death.

But the little red hen lives yet in her house at the edge of the wood by herself.

THE ROBBER FOX AND HIS MOTHER

REYNARD'S RIDE

One DAY BRUIN, the bear, killed a horse. Afterward he was eating him when Reynard, the fox, happened along.

"Ah!" Reynard said to himself, "here is Bruin feasting while I am wandering about hungry. That horse looks good to me. I must scheme to get a taste of him."

He walked on softly, passed behind Bruin, then turned and jumped to the other side of the horse.

Bruin looked up and growled, but quick as a flash Reynard snapped a mouthful of the meat and ran off.

"Don't be in a hurry," Bruin called after him. "Come back and I'll tell you how you can get a horse all for your own eating." Reynard wanted very much to know how to do that, and he returned, but he did not go very close to Bruin, for he did not wholly trust him. He stopped at a safe distance and said, "Now tell me."

"Well," Bruin responded, "just search around until you find a horse out at pasture lying asleep in the sunshine. Then bind yourself fast to him by tying the hair of his tail to your brush. After that make your teeth meet in the flesh of his thigh. He may prance around a little, but hang on, and when the horse is dead you can eat him at your leisure."

"Thank you," the fox said. "I think that is a very good plan." And away he went to the pastures where the farmers let their horses graze. He kept a sharp lookout until he found a horse asleep in the sunshine. Without delay he knotted the long hair of the horse's tail firmly to his brush. Then he made his teeth meet in the horse's thigh.

The horse, gave a startled cry of pain, sprang to his feet, and began to kick and rear. Reynard at first kept his grip, but he lost it when the horse set off for a wild gallop about the pasture. He was dashed against the earth and the stones, and he got more battered and bruised every minute. In the midst of the frantic race the horse nearly ran over Jack Longears, the rabbit. Jack leaped out of the way just in time to save himself.

"Where are you going so fast, Reynard?" he called.

"Never mind where," Reynard cried. "I'm going posthaste on business of life and death."

Jack stood up on his hind legs, and laughed till his sides ached, it was so funny to see Reynard ride posthaste.

Luckily for Reynard, he at last broke loose, and he was limping away to his den in the forest when he met

Bruin. He let the bear have all the road and turned well out to one side. If Bruin had not hailed him he would have gone along without speaking.

"Hello! Reynard," Bruin said, "what is the matter with you? You look as if you had crawled through a knothole backward."

"You can laugh," Reynard retorted, "but would have you know that I have been doing nothing except to ride posthaste."

Bruin would have talked more, but Reynard hobbled along into the forest without saying another word. He could not help acknowledging that Bruin had out-witted him, and since then he has had no desire to catch a horse for himself.

THE FOX AND THE WOLF'S DAUGHTER

There WAS ONCE a wolf who had a beautiful and clever daughter. She was the finest girl in the country, and all the men animals who did not already have partners came courting her. It made her proud to have so many to pick from, but she was a lively creature, and though she smiled on every one of them she turned up her nose if a beau wanted to stop courting and go to keeping house.

"No," she would say, "I am not ready yet to settle down like my mother."

By and by her old daddy got exasperated with all the foolishness. He had been kept awake night after night by the giggling and chaffing of the young people. They were sitting in his best armchairs and wearing them out when they ought to have been sleeping and getting strength to flax around and earn their living the next day.

So one morning he said to his daughter: "You must choose the man you like best and start a home of your own. I'm not going to have you trotting around anymore and fetching company here to eat our food[1] and be waited on by your mother."

When he said that, the girl sniffed and pouted, but she knew she must do as he ordered. After a while she told him he might get ready whatever he was going to give her for a wedding present.

"Who are you going to marry?" he asked. She blushed and dropped her eyes. "I think young Mr. Fox is a mighty nice man," she said.

"Well," the old wolf growled, "it's true enough that he's a sweet talker. He can't be beat when it comes to courting the girls." The wolf was not overmuch pleased, but he said no more, and he let it be known that Mr. Fox would soon marry his daughter. The wedding was to be a grand affair, and all hands went to work to get ready for it.

In the midst of the preparations young Mr. Fox called at Mr. Wolf's house and began to brag about his wedding clothes. "I've been to the tailor," he said, "and I've told him to make as fine a suit as he knows how. The clothes are to have pretty shiny buttons on 'em. There'll be two rows down the front of the coat and some on the sleeves, and I told the tailor to put a

[1] Originally "victuals".

button here —"

He started to reach around to the back of his coat, but at that moment a big flea gave him a terrible bite on his knee. He could not help clapping his hand to the spot. Fleas are very bad in the wolf houses, but the wolves do not like to have any one say so. They get angry if a visitor shows that he has been bitten. Mr. Fox knew how touchy they were on that subject, and when he grabbed for the flea he pretended he was just showing where a button was going to be.

Then he went on to say, "And I told the tailor to put a button here —"

Again he was about to point around to the back of his coat when the flea nipped him in the ribs, and he had to make a clutch there without delay. He cleared his throat and tried once more to show where the button was to be. "I'm going to have a button herem: he said, but the flea pinched him on the neck.

No sooner had he slapped that place and resumed his story than he got a bite on the hip. The bites continued, and he kept putting the buttons here and there till he was wild with confusion and discomfort, and he had scratched almost everywhere.

Finally the flea gave him a most savage bite on the nose just as he was telling where a button was going, and he could not help clawing the spot.

Meanwhile old Mr. Wolf had been getting madder

and madder right straight along, and when Mr. Fox said he was going to have a button on the end of his nose he could hold in his wrath no longer.

"Hi!" he exclaimed, "I can prove now that I made no mistake when I said you were an idiot while you were courting my daughter. I haven't been at all anxious to welcome you into my family from the start. But I gave in to the girl and her mother. Now, though, I take my stand, and all the women-folks in the world can't persuade me to have a son-in-law who wants to look as if toadstools were growing all over him. Put a button on your nose if you want to, but you are not going to carry it into a house you share with my daughter."

Then he flung open the door and drove Mr. Fox out, and he was so angry he would not listen to a word from Mr. Fox, or Mr. Fox's kinsfolk, or the neighbors, or his wife, or the girl. The next week he got his daughter married to the leanest old timber wolf that ever drew breath, and since that time he has not had a thing to do with any fox whatever.

MR. WOLF GETS ANGRY AT MR. FOX

THE SLEEPING FOX AND THE BOY WITH A STONE

Once UPON A TIME there was a little boy who lived with his father and mother on a farm in the midst of a forest. The nearest village was on the borders of the forest three miles away. It was there that the family went to market, and it was there that they went to church.

One Sunday the little boy's father was sick, and when it was time to start for church the little boy's mother called him to her and said: "This time you can go to church alone. Your father is not well, and I must stay at home to take care of him. But you know the way as well as we do."

"Oh, yes! " the little boy said, " I know the way perfectly, and this is a nice sunny morning. If you will brush my hair, I will put on my best hat and coat, and start. I heard the church bell ringing a little while ago when I drove our cow to pasture."

So his mother brushed his hair, and he put on his

best coat and hat, and left home for the long walk through the forest to church. At one place on the road was a clearing where the choppers had been at work and not far from the highway was a rock on which a fox lay sleeping.

By and by the little boy came walking along, and when he was opposite the rock he saw the fox lying there in the sunshine fast asleep. He stopped and looked at the fox and thought a moment. Then he picked up a good-sized stone and prepared to throw it at the sleeping Reynard.

"I will kill that fox," he said. "Afterward I can have his skin, and I will sell it. I shall get money for the skin — yes, a great deal of money — and with the money I intend to buy some rye. I shall sow the rye in one of my father's fields. When it has begun to grow and has made the field all green, people who are on their way to church will stop to look at it, and they will say, 'Oh, what splendid rye that boy has got!'

"Then I shall shout to them, 'Hello, there! Keep away from my rye!'

"But they won't hear me, and I shall shout again louder, 'Hello, there! Keep away from my rye!'

"But still they won't pay any attention to me. So I shall scream with all my might, 'Keep away from my rye!'

"Then they will listen to me."

However the boy had screamed so loud that the fox waked up and sprang to his feet. Reynard only paused to give one startled look toward the boy, and scampered off into the forest. He vanished so quickly that the boy never even threw the stone at him. There is an old saying: —

"It's always best to take what you can reach, And not of undone deeds to loudly screech. "

If the little boy had known this old saying and re-membered it, I might have had a very different story to tell.

The Fox Who Did Not Want to be a Heathen

Once THERE WAS a goose who lived beside a lake. Sometimes she paddled about on the water. Sometimes she dived down under the surface. Sometimes she waddled along the marshy borders of the lake hunting for frogs.

She found plenty to eat, and she grew fatter every day. But the fatter she became, the less inclined she was to exert herself. So she spent much of her time on a sunny slope near the lake, asleep, with her head under her wing.

In the wood, not far away, dwelt a cunning red fox. One day, as he was prowling about, he saw the goose asleep on that sunny bank which she found so comfortable.

"Ha! " he said, "what a fat goose! Here's a chance for a good supper."

He crept closer, made a sudden leap, and the

goose awakened to find herself held fast by one of her wings. She struggled to get free, and she honked and hissed loudly, but the fox only laughed at her.

"It's of no use making such a fuss," he told her. "You can't scare me by your honking and hissing, and you can't get away. I'm going to eat you right here."

"Well, if you are going to do that," the goose said, "I hope you will do it decently and not forget your manners."

"Forget my manners?" Reynard said. "I don't understand what you mean. Please explain. Now if you had me in your mouth as I have you, tell me what you would do."

"You are a heathen, Reynard," the goose declared. "Good Christians ask a blessing on their food before they eat. If I had caught you as you have caught me, I certainly would not eat you until I had folded my hands, shut my eyes and said a grace. I would be ashamed to gobble you down without doing that. Thank goodness! I've been better brought up than to do such a thing."

"God forbid that I should be a heathen!" the fox exclaimed. "You have the right idea of what is proper. To be sure, I am eager to eat you, for I see plainly that you are both plump and tender, but I quite agree with you that one ought not to neglect his manners." So he folded his hands, shut his eyes, and with a very demure look on his countenance repeated a pious grace. But while he expressed his thankfulness for the ample size and toothsome fatness of his captive, and asked a blessing on the bountiful repast of which he was about to partake, the goose waddled softly away. However, she had only gone a short distance when he finished his grace and opened his eyes. No time was to be lost, and the goose spread her wings for a flight.

"Good-bye!" she called back to the fox as she left the ground. "I like your manners. Ihope your supper will agree with you." She flew far out over the lake and let herself splash down on the water. Then she floated and rested after the exertion of flying and the excitement of her narrow escape.

The fox was left to lick his lips in vain regret. "Ah!" he said in disgust, "I will learn a lesson from this. Never again in all my life will I say a grace 'til after I feel the meat warm in my stomach."

THE LIMPING FOX

Once UPON A TIME there was a man whose right eye always smiled, and whose left eye always cried. This man had three sons, two of them very clever and the third very stupid. When these sons grew up, they were curious to know why their father's eyes were so unlike the eyes of other people. They could not puzzle out any reason for it, and one day when they were together in the garden talking the matter over, the eldest son said: "Why should we allow this uncertainty to continue to trouble us? I will ask our father to explain the mystery."

So he marched into the house and said to his father, "I would very much like to know why one of your eyes always smiles and the other always weeps."

But his father, instead of answering, became very angry and ordered the son out of the house. The young fellow ran to the garden and joined his brothers.

"What did he say?" they asked anxiously.

"You had better go yourselves, if you want to find out," was all the reply he gave them.

Then the second son entered the house and asked his father the same question the eldest son had asked. Again the father became angry, and he commanded the questioner to leave the house. The youth returned to his brothers and said to the youngest, "It is your turn now to try your luck."

The simpleton did not hesitate. He marched boldly in to his father and said: "My brothers will not tell me what answer you gave them when they asked you about your eyes. Will you please tell me why they are not like those of other people?"

As before, the father was furious and ordered the son out of the house. But the simpleton would not go. He was sure he had nothing to fear from his father.

Soon the old man ceased threatening and said: "I see that you have courage, and I will satisfy your curiosity. My right eye laughs because I am glad to have a son like you, and my left eye weeps because a precious treasure has been stolen from me. I formerly had in my garden a vine that yielded a ton of grapes every day, but someone carried it off, and I have wept over its loss ever since."

The simpleton went out to his brothers and repeated what his father had said. Then they all decided to start without delay in search of the wonderful vine.

At first they traveled together, but by and by they came to where the road parted. the two elder brothers took one way, and the simpleton the other.

"Thank goodness he decided to go on by himself!" the eldest brother said. "He never would have been of any help in finding the magic vine."

"That he would not," the second brother agreed, "and now let us eat some of the food we have brought along."

They sat down by the roadside and were eating when a lame fox came out of a piece of woodland that was near by and begged them to give him a portion of their food. But they jumped up and chased him away with their canes. The fox limped off on three feet, and he hurried on til he came to where the simpleton had sat down to eat beside the other road.

"Sir," the fox said, "can you spare me a crust of bread?"

"I have only a very little bread," the simpleton replied, "but you shall have half of it."

"Where are you going, brother?" the fox asked when he had finished his share of the food.

So the youth told about his father; and of the wonderful vine, which he himself was now seeking.

"Dear me, how lucky that you and I met!" the fox said. "I know what has become of that vine. Follow me."

So they went on till they drew near to a large garden. "The vine for which you are searching is in this garden," the fox said, "but it is very stoutly guarded. You must listen carefully to what I say and heed my directions. You will have to pass through twelve gates before you reach the vine, and at each gate are posted two armed sentinels. But you will find the gates open and the sentinels asleep. Go on without fear, and when you get to the vine you will see two shovels near it, one of wood and the other of iron. Be sure to use the wooden shovel to dig up the vine, for the iron shovel would make a noise and rouse the sentinels. Then they would slam the gates shut and capture you."

"I will do as you say," the young man promised.

He passed safely through the twelve gates and found the vine and the shovels, but he thought it would be impossible to dig the hard earth with the wooden shovel, and he picked up the iron one. Scarcely had he started digging when he struck some stones, and the noise wakened the guards. Instantly they banged the gates shut and came running to the vine. Then they seized the simpleton and dragged him off to their master.

"Why did you try to steal my vine that yields a ton of grapes a day?" the owner of the garden demanded.

"The vine is not yours," the simpleton asserted

stoutly. "It belongs to my father, and if you will not give it to me now, I warn you that I shall scheme to get it somehow, sooner or later."

"Well," the man said, "you shall have the vine, if you will bring me in exchange an apple off the apple tree that blossoms every twenty-four hours and bears fruit of gold."

Then he gave orders that the simpleton should be released. The guards carried the youth outside of the grounds, and as soon as they set him free, he hurried off to consult the fox.

"Now you see what comes of not following my advice," the fox said. "I am much displeased. However, I will help you. Come, we will go to the garden where the wonderful tree is growing. The owner has guarded the tree just as the vine was guarded, but there, too, the gates are open and the sentinels sleeping. Near the tree you will find two poles, one of gold and the other of wood. Take the wooden pole, and you will be able to knock off an apple without making any noise."

They went to the garden and near its outer gate the simpleton parted from the fox. Then he went on alone and soon arrived at the apple tree, but he was so dazzled by the sight of the beautiful golden fruit that he quite forgot all that the fox had said. He seized the golden pole and struck a branch a sounding blow.

At once the guards awoke, slammed the gates

shut, caught the simpleton, and took him to their master. He told his story, and the owner of the garden said, "You shall have a golden apple if you will bring me in exchange the golden horse that can go around the world in twenty-four hours."

The simpleton was allowed to depart, and he rejoined the fox. This time the fox was angry, and no wonder: "If you had only done as I directed," he said, "you would be at home with your father by this time. You don't deserve anymore help. Nevertheless, I will tell you how to get the swift horse. He is in a stable in the neighboring forest closely guarded, but you will find the guards asleep. Near his stall hang two halters, one of gold, the other of hemp. Put the hempen halter on him, for if you attempt to use the golden halter to lead him away he will begin neighing and will waken the guards."

The simpleton found the golden horse, and the two halters. "What a beautiful creature!" the youth exclaimed. "Surely the fox would not have me put a hempen halter on a creature like that. No, no!"

So he used the golden halter, and the horse began to neigh loudly. That brought the guards, and the simpleton was conducted to their master and told his story.

"You shall have the horse," the owner said, "if you will bring me in exchange a golden maiden who has never yet seen either the sun or the moon."

"But if I am to bring you the golden maiden," the simpleton responded, "you must lend me the golden steed to ride on in my search for her."

"Very well," the man agreed, and the youth rode away on the golden horse to consult the fox.

He had again disobeyed the fox's orders, yet the fox once more aided him. "Follow me," the fox said, after the simpleton had told him of the new quest he was obliged to make. "The maiden dwells in a mountain grotto, and she has never been outside of it to see either the sun by day or the moon by night."

Presently they reached the grotto, and the young man rode in on the golden horse, and there he found a beautiful maiden all of gold. He placed her on the horse and led the steed out of the grotto to where the fox was waiting.

"Are you not sorry to give such a lovely maiden in exchange for a horse?" the fox asked. "Perhaps I could manage to take her place."

So saying, the fox transformed himself into another golden maiden so like the first that it was difficult to tell which was which. They left the maiden of the grotto where she was and went to the owner of the horse. He accepted the fox maiden, and the youth took the golden horse to the owner of the golden apples and received one of the apples in exchange. Then he went and gave the apple for his father's magic vine, and carried the vine home. Lastly he returned to the mountain grotto and got the beautiful golden maiden, and he took her to his father's house and married her.

How Mrs. Fox Married Again

There WAS ONCE a lady fox whose husband died, and after he was buried she retired to her room and locked herself in. There she stayed day after day and week after week for a long time. She had a cat for a servant, and this servant kept the house tidy and cooked the meals.

At length a suitor came knocking at the door. The cat went to see who was there and found a wolf standing on the doorstep. He bowed very politely and said: —

"Good-day, Miss Cat, so brisk and gay,
Pray, tell me why alone you stay
And what it is you cook today? "

The cat answered: —

> *"I am melting some butter and warm-*
> *ing some beer. Won't you kindly come*
> *in and partake of my cheer? "*

The wolf bowed again and said: —

> *"I thank you very much, Miss Cat,*
> *Most gladly will I do just that;**
> *And while I eat, pray, go and see*
> *If Mrs. Fox will welcome me."*

The cat said: —

> *"She is sitting upstairs in her grief,*
> *And her eyes with her weeping are*
> *sore.*
> *From her sorrow she gets no relief*
> *Now that poor Mr. Fox is no more."*
>
> *"Won't she take another spouse*
> *To protect her and her house?"*

the wolf asked.

> *"I will go and find out*
> *So you'll know without doubt," —*

the cat replied.
Then she ran upstairs, pit-a-pat, pit-a-pat, And knocked at the door, rat-a-tat, rat-a-tat!

**"Mrs. Fox, my lady fair,
Tell me, please, if you are there,"**

she said.

**"Yes, I'm here, my pussy dear,
Where I've been for half a year,"**

Mrs. Fox answered.

**"There's a suitor below.
Shall I tell him to go?"**

the cat said.

Mrs. Fox opened the door and asked, "Does the gentleman wear red breeches, and has he a pointed nose?"

"No," the cat answered.

"Then I won't have him," Mrs. Fox declared. "Send him away."

So the cat went downstairs and sent the wolf away.

A few days later a dog came to woo the lady fox. The cat went to her mistress's room to announce him, and Mrs. Fox asked, "Does he wear red breeches, and has he a pointed nose?"

"No," the cat said.

"Send him away, then," Mrs. Fox ordered. Another day a bear came, but his breeches and his nose were not satisfactory, and he had no better luck than the others.

Not long afterward a lion called, and he, too, was sent away, and for the same reason.

At last a fox came to court Mrs. Fox, and when she learned from the cat that he wore red breeches and had a pointed nose she said, "Then I will have him, and you must make haste to prepare the wedding feast."

So the cat caught as many mice as she could in celebration of the happy event, and got ready a fine feast, and swept out the house. Presently the wedding took place with mirth, dancing, and rejoicing; and as I have never heard anything to the contrary, perhaps the bride and groom and their guests are dancing yet.

A FOX COMES TO COURT MRS. FOX

The Fox and the Boastful Rooster

Once UPON A TIME there was a rooster who was very proud of his strong legs and bright feathers and red comb. But most of all he was proud of his powerful voice. As he strutted around the barnyard he stopped every now and then to crow and to say to himself, "I am the handsomest rooster in all the world, and no other rooster lives who can crow as loud as I can."

One morning, while he was strutting around as usual and making more noise than all the rest of the barnyard people put together, the brown hen came and spoke to him.

"What a lovely day this is," she said. "The sun shines bright, and all the birds are singing. Let us fly over the fence and hunt for worms in the garden."

"Alright," the rooster agreed. And they flew over the fence and hurried away to the garden.

It so happened that a sly old fox was lurking near by. He saw the rooster and said to himself, "That fellow is just what I want for my dinner. I wish he would come over here where I am hiding in the bushes so I could pounce on him. But there he is scratching around in the middle of the garden. I shall have to go out in the open and speak to him."

So the fox walked toward the rooster. However, the rooster and the hen saw him coming, and they were careful to keep at a safe distance.

"Don't be afraid, Mr. Rooster," the fox said; "I want to have a friendly chat with you."

"Alright," the rooster responded; "I don't object to visiting with you, if only you don't come any nearer."

"Your suspicions hurt my feelings," the fox said. "But never mind. I wanted to ask you how many tricks you could do."

"I can do three tricks," the rooster replied. "How many can you do?"

"Seventy-three[2]," the fox declared.

"Can you? I wouldn't have thought it," the rooster said; "and what is the best one of all?"

"It is one my grandfather taught me," the fox answered. "He could shut both eyes and give a great shout, and I learned to do the same thing."

"Why, that's nothing! I could do that myself," the rooster bragged.

[2] Originally "Threescore and thirteen"; threescore meaning sixty as the animals are counting in an archaic fashion

"Do you really think you could?" the fox asked. "Try it."

So the rooster swelled out his breast and crowed as loud as he could, "Cock-a- doodle-do." And then he flapped his wings as if he had done a great thing. But he had only shut one eye, for he wanted to watch the fox with the other.

"Very pretty," the fox commented, "almost as pretty as when the parson preaches in church. However, you didn't shut both eyes. I hardly thought you could do the trick as well as my grandfather did."

"Yes I can, too," the rooster affirmed, and he forgot the need of caution, closed both eyes, and crowed, "Cock-a-doodle—" But he never finished the crow, for as soon as his eyes were shut, the sly fox leaped forward, gripped him by the neck and started to run to the woods.

The brown hen at once gave chase, crying: "Let go of that rooster! He belongs to me!"

"Mr. Fox," the rooster said, "that brown hen can go very swift. Do you know what it is to be henpecked? I do, and it is far from pleasant, I assure you. If you don't want her to catch up with us and peck you, I advise you to call back: 'This rooster is not yours. He is mine.'"

The fox found it slow work lugging along the heavy rooster, and he did not wish to be pecked. He thought the plan the rooster suggested was a very good one, and he opened his mouth to shout back to the hen that the rooster was his.

But by so doing he let go his grip on the captive's neck, and no sooner did the rooster find himself at liberty than he flew up into a tree. Then he shut both eyes and gave a loud crow, and that is all there is to this story.

REYNARD AND THE FOXHUNTER

Once UPON A TIME there was a foxhunter who lived all alone in a hut near a forest. He came home one evening, tired after a long day spent in hunting, started a fire in his fireplace, and then sat down and fell asleep in his chair.

By and by he awoke, and was surprised to see a fox sitting comfortably at the side of the fire. Reynard had come in at a hole under the door provided for the convenience of the dog, the cat, the pig, and the hens. It was a chilly autumn evening, and he had evidently visited the hut to get warm.

"Oho!" the foxhunter exclaimed, "here is a fox right in my own house. Well, Mr. Fox, here you'll stay til I have a chance to rap you over the head. The hole under the door is your only chance to escape, and I'll see that you don't get out there."

Then he sat down on the floor with his back

against the hole.

"Ah!" the fox said to himself, "I'll soon make that stupid fellow get up."

, So he searched around til he found the man's shoes, and he picked them up with his teeth and dropped them into the fire. "Hurry!" he said to the fox-hunter; "jump up and save your shoes!"

"I shan't get up for that, my fine gentleman," the foxhunter responded stubbornly.

"Then I'll try again," the fox said.

He soon found the man's stockings and put them in the fire. "You'll have to be quick if you want to save them," he said to the man.

"I shan't get up for that, my fine gentleman," the foxhunter declared.

So the fox made another exploring trip around the room and found the man's overcoat. He brought it and pushed it into the fire. "You'll be cold when winter comes if you don't have that coat," he said to the man. "Hurry, and rescue it."

"I shan't get up for that, my fine gentleman," the foxhunter persisted.

"I'm not through with you yet," the fox retorted.

He next dragged the man's best trousers across the floor and fed them to the flames. "Surely, you can't afford to lose those," he said to the man. "Hustle over here and save them."

"I shan't get up for that, my fine gentleman," the foxhunter said.

"I don't see much left in the hut except your straw bed," the fox remarked. "We'll see how you like having that burned."

He tugged at the bed until he got it to the fire. Then he pushed it in. "Now will you get up?" the fox cried.

The flames flared hot and high and crackled fiercely, and the hut was filled with smoke.

"That is more than I can stand!" the man shouted, and he jumped up in great alarm.

Now the fox had the chance he had been working for. So he took advantage of the confusion and slipped out of the hole under the door and ran off into the forest.

THE FOX AND THE
OLD CAT AND DOG

There WAS ONCE a man and his wife who had an old cat and an old dog. One day the man, whose name was Simon, said to his wife, whose name was Susan: "Why should we continue to keep our old cat? She never catches any mice nowadays. I have made up my mind to drown her."

But his wife said: "Don't do that. I think she can still catch mice."

"Rubbish!" Simon exclaimed. "The mice might dance on her, and she could never catch one. No, I will put her in a bag and drown her."

Susan was very sorrowful when she heard him say that, and so was the cat, who had been sitting under the table listening to the conversation. Simon went out to the barn to get a bag, and at once the cat began to *miaow* and look up beseechingly into the face of her mistress. This was more than Susan could bear, and she opened the door and said, "Fly for your life, you poor beast, and get well away from here before your master returns."

The cat took her advice and ran as fast as she could into the forest, and when Simon brought his bag into the house his wife told him that the cat had vanished.

"So much the better for her," was Simon's comment; "and now that she is out of the way we must consider what to do with our old dog. He is so nearly blind and deaf that he is worse than useless. He always barks when there is no need, and makes not a sound when he ought to bark. I think I shall have to shoot him."

But the soft-hearted Susan said: "Surely he is not as useless as you imagine; and remember how long and faithfully he has served us. We can very well afford to take care of him for the rest of his life."

"Don't be foolish," her husband responded. "The courtyard might be full of thieves, and he would never know it. Besides, no thief would be afraid of him, for he has not a tooth in his head. If he has served us, he has had his food every day to pay for it. No, it's all up with him. I am going to the shed to load my gun, and then I'll take him out and shoot him."

Susan was very unhappy at these words, and so was the dog, who was lying in a corner of the room and had heard everything. As soon as the man went to the shed, the old dog stood up and howled so mournfully that Susan opened the door, and said, "Fly for your life, you poor beast." And the dog ran off to the forest with his tail between his legs.

When Simon came in Susan said to him, "The dog has disappeared."

"That's lucky for him," Simon remarked, but his wife sighed. She had been very fond of the old dog, and though she was glad he had escaped she did not like to think of his wandering around homeless.

It happened that the dog and cat met each other in the forest. They had not been the best of friends at home, but each was glad of the other's company there in the lonely woodland. They sat down under a tree and were relating their woes to one another when a fox came along. He saw the two disconsolate creatures sitting there talking over their sad fate, and he asked them what they were grumbling about.

The cat replied, "I have caught no end of mice in my day, but now that I am old and past work my master wants to drown me."

"As for me," the dog said, "many a night have I watched and guarded my master's house, but now that I am old and deaf he wants to shoot me."

"That's the way of the world," the fox commented. "However, I will help you to regain your master's favor if you will first help me in my own troubles."

They promised to do their best, and the fox said: "The wolf has declared war against me, and is at this moment marching to fight me supported by a bear and a wild boar. Tomorrow there will be a fierce battle between us."

"I haven't the least desire to do any fighting," the dog responded, "but I will stand by you."

"Yes, and so will I," the cat said. "If we are killed, it at any rate is better to die on the field of battle than to perish ignobly at home."

They shook paws with the fox and concluded the bargain. Then the fox sent a message to the wolf naming a certain place where he and the cat and dog would be on the morrow ready for the battle.

Early the next day the three friends set forth to encounter the fox's enemies. But the wolf, the bear, and the wild boar arrived on the spot first. When they had waited some time for the fox and his allies, the bear said, "I will climb up into the great oak that grows here, and perhaps I can see them coming."

Up he scrambled, and after looking around, he said: "Ah! There they are off in the distance marching in this direction like a mighty army. They seem to be carrying a great sword. No, it is not a sword, but the tail of the cat. She is lame and limps on three legs and I suppose holds her tail erect from pain."

The bear and his companions laughed and jeered and made merry over the appearance of their enemies and did not doubt that they could easily vanquish them. It was a warm day, and presently the bear said: "The heat makes me sleepy. We shall have to wait here for those fellows a long time at the rate they are coming. I'm going to curl myself up in the fork of the tree and have a nap."

The wolf thought he also would have a nap, and he lay down under the tree. Then the wild boar decided to make himself comfortable by creeping into a heap of dead leaves, where he covered himself so that no portion of him was in sight except one ear.

They were all asleep when the fox, the dog, and the cat arrived. Just then the boar chanced to twitch his exposed ear. The cat saw it and thought it was a mouse. Immediately she made a spring and fastened her claws and teeth into it. At this the boar leaped up in a dreadful fright, gave one loud grunt of dismay, and scampered off into the woodland.

The cat was no less startled than the boar. She spit with terror and scrambled up the tree right into the face of the bear. Now it was the bear's turn to be alarmed, and with a startled growl he half jumped and half fell out of the oak. He came down on the wolf and killed him as dead as a stone. But the bear did not stop to find out how badly the wolf was hurt. He made all haste to escape into the forest.

The fox had won the battle, and he said to his companions, "You can now return to your old home and I will go with you and try to make you welcome."

On the way he caught a score of mice. When he and the cat and the dog reached Simon's cottage he laid the mice down beside the door and said to the cat, "Take in one mouse after another and lay them down before your master."

"I will do whatever you tell me to do," the cat agreed.

It was just after sundown, the day's work was done, and Simon and his wife were sitting at the fireside. The cat brought in the twenty mice, one at a time, and laid them at the man's feet.

Then Susan said to her husband, "Just look, here is our old cat back again, and see what a lot of mice she has caught."

"Wonders will never cease!" Simon exclaimed. "I certainly thought the old cat would never catch another mouse."

"Well," Susan remarked, "I always said our cat was a most excellent creature, but you men think you know best."

Meanwhile the fox said to the dog: "Your master has recently killed a pig. When the night gets a little darker, you must go into the courtyard and bark with all your might just as if the pork were being stolen."

"Alright," the dog said. And after he had waited about half an hour he went into the courtyard and began to bark loudly.

"Our dog must have come back," Susan said to her husband, "for I hear him barking. Do go out and see what is the matter. Perhaps thieves are stealing our sausages."

But Simon said, "The foolish beast is as deaf as a post and is always barking at nothing." And he would not go out to investigate.

The next morning Susan got up early to get ready to go to church in a neighboring town, and she thought she would take some sausages to her aunt who lived there. But when she went to her larder she found a great hole in the floor, and all the sausages were gone.

"Simon!" she called to her husband, "thieves have been here last night, and they have not left a single sausage. You see I was perfectly right about the warning our old dog gave us. Oh! If you had only gone out when I asked you to!"

Simon scratched his head and said: "I can't understand this thing. I did not think it possible that the old dog was so quick at hearing."

"Ah!" Susan said, "I have told you again and again that our old dog was the best dog in the world, but as usual you thought you knew better than I did! Why is it that men are so unreasonable?"

After that the cat and the dog were restored to favor. They were satisfied, and Simon and Susan were satisfied, and so was the fox, for he had carried away the sausages.

THE TWO FOXES
AND THE HOT ROLLS

TWO FOXES lay at the edge of some woods near a roadway. One was a big fox, and the other was a little fox. They were wondering how they could get something to eat. It was winter time and the snow whitened all the earth. Not a blade of grass was to be seen, and not a bird or a mouse stirred in the fields.

"This is hungry weather," the big fox said. "I feel as hollow as an eggshell."

"So do I," the little fox said. "I'm hungry enough to eat my own ears if I could reach them. Let us hunt for game in the forest."

"Oh, no! That would be too much like work," the big fox objected. "We will fare just as well if we wait here and depend on our wits."

Pretty soon they saw a peasant girl walking along the road with a basket on her back, and out of the basket came a very pleasant smell—the smell of hot rolls.

"That girl is bringing us our dinner," the big fox said.

"I think not," the little fox sighed. "She is going right along past. She doesn't know we are here."

"The girl needs to be taught a lesson," the big fox declared. "She has our dinner in that basket she is carrying, and we must make her give it to us."

"But how can you make her do that?" the little fox asked.

"We will hurry to get ahead of her," the big fox replied. "Then you lie down in the road and pretend to be dead. The girl will put down her basket to take you up, and I will leap forward and run off with the basket. Those rolls will make us a splendid feast."

"Very well," the little fox agreed; "I can do my part if you can do yours."

So they ran in a roundabout way through the woods till they had gone far enough to get into the road ahead of the girl without being seen. The big fox hid behind a snowdrift, and the little fox lay down in the road.

Presently the girl came along and saw the fox stretched out there motionless. She stopped and looked at him and poked him with her cane.

"Oho!" she exclaimed, "I'm in luck today. Here's a dead fox, and he is a nice, sleek beast whose skin will sell for a good bit of money."

She put down the basket and stooped to pick up the little fox. But that instant the big fox snatched up the basket and scampered off with it. The girl turned away from the little fox to see what was going on, and in a twinkling he came to life and followed his companion.

But the big fox ran on ahead and showed quite plainly that he meant to keep the rolls all to himself. At length he came to a blacksmith's shop and stopped, and the little fox joined him. A horse was tied at the door, and the horse was shod with golden shoes. The foxes noticed that one of the shoes had a name on it.

"Come," the big fox said to his companion, "let us go near and see what is written on that shoe."

"No, I will not go," the little fox responded, "for I do not know how to read."

"Then I will go alone," the big fox said. "I never saw a name on a horseshoe before, and I am curious to learn what it is."

But when he drew near, the horse lifted the foot on which was the golden shoe with a name on it and gave the fox a kick that killed him.

"Ah!" the little fox said, "I am glad that I am no scholar." And he went off with all the rolls.

THE PEASANT GIRL THINKS
SHE HAS FOUND A DEAD FOX

A Fox and His Friends

IN A CERTAIN VILLAGE there was once a man whose whole property consisted of the house he dwelt in, a horse, a greyhound, and a gun. His only occupation was hunting, and he depended on the game he shot for his living.

One fine day he took his gun and called his dog, mounted his horse, and set off to hunt. He went up among the high mountains, and after riding a long distance, he reached a little open valley. On its far side he tied his horse to a tree, and walked forward into the thick woods with his gun on his shoulder, and his dog by his side.

All day the man hunted, but he only killed a single deer. When he returned with it to the little valley he was astonished to see a fox lying in the grass beside his horse. He raised his gun to shoot the creature, but Reynard, who had observed what the man was about, sprang quickly to his feet and said imploringly: "For the love of Heaven, spare my life! Let me be your servant. I will do your bidding faithfully and will guard your horse while you are hunting."

The man took pity on the fox and said, "Alright, you can go home with me, and you shall be well treated as long as you do as you have promised to do."

Then he laid the deer across the horse in front of the saddle, mounted, and returned to the village, with his dog and the fox running along at the horse's heels. After he reached home he skinned the deer, put away such portions of it as he wanted to eat, and threw the rest to the fox.

The night passed, and in the first dawn of morning the man again set out. He took the fox with him and went to the same high valley to which he had gone the day previous. There he tied his horse and left the fox to guard him while he went into the forest to hunt.

By and by a bear came along and saw the horse and would have killed and devoured him, but the fox said: "I beg you not to harm this horse. He belongs to a hunter who is my master. Stay with me till the hunter returns, and he will allow you to become his servant and will take us both to his home and feed us."

"If that is so he is just such a master as I would like to have," the bear said joyfully, and he lay down beside the fox to await the man's return.

Late in the day the man came out of the woods carrying two deer that he had killed. He was much surprised to see a bear lying there with the fox, and he threw down the deer and hastily took aim at the bear with his gun. But the fox sprang forward and said: "I beseech you, good sir, to spare this bear's life. Take him home with you, and he will keep me company in guarding your horse, and he will aid you in every need and danger."

"Very well," the man said, "it shall be as you wish."

Then he adjusted the two deer across his horse and rode home in high good humor, accompanied by the fox and the bear.

On the following day he again went hunting in the mountains and left his horse in the same little valley. The fox and the bear had come too, and they stayed with the horse as guards. While the man was roaming in the forest with his gun and his dog, a wolf saw the horse and would have sprung on him had not the fox interposed.

"Do this horse no injury," the fox said. "This bear and I are here to protect him, and he belongs to our master. I advise you to join us in serving the owner of the horse. He will take you to his house and feed and lodge you."

"Then I will be his servant," the wolf said.

The man presently came back to the valley, and he would have shot the wolf had not the fox leaped forward and explained that the wolf intended to serve him. This time he had three of the wild creatures of the forest following him when he went home.

The next day he rode forth and climbed once more to the remote valley in the mountains, and there he left his three servants guarding his horse. While he was hunting this time a great bird of the desert came soaring over the forest heights. The bird spied the hunter's steed and swooped down to carry him off, but the fox entreated the bird not to harm the horse and urged him to join the other animals in serving the horse's master.

The bird of the desert agreed to do as the fox suggested, and they all went home with the man, and he fed and took care of them.

They lived very happily with him and always accompanied him when he went hunting. One day the fox said to his companions: "See here, my friends, we must provide a wife for our worthy master."

"Good!" the others exclaimed, "but how shall we go about it? We do not know where to find any suitable maiden for him."

"The emperor has a daughter," Reynard said. "Let us get her for our master. Bird of the Desert, I think you had better attempt the task while the rest of us remain here. Set off at once for the imperial castle, and after you arrive watch until the princess goes out for a walk. Then seize her and bring her back with you."

So the bird of the desert spread his broad wings,

and away he flew to the imperial castle. There he alighted in a tall tree and watched for the emperor's daughter. Just at nightfall she and her waiting-woman came out of the castle and started for a walk. But in one swoop the bird of the desert flapped down to where she was, put her on his back, and flew with her to the home of his master.

The princess was beautiful and amiable, and the hunter was youthful and clever, and they soon grew very fond of each other. Everything progressed as well as the fox and his friends could have desired, and presently the wedding was celebrated.

Meanwhile there was great consternation at the imperial castle. The emperor was much distressed to have his daughter carried off, and he offered a rich reward to whoever should bring her safely home, but for some time no one would undertake the adventure. Then a gypsy woman presented herself before the emperor. "Your Highness," she said, "if your daughter still lives, I think I can find her."

"Hurrah!" the emperor cried out in delight, "and as soon as you bring her here to me you shall have the rich reward."

The gypsy woman went home, and by her en-chantments learned that the princess was distant ten days' journey at the home of the hunter. In order to go there she decided to use a magic rug that was in her possession. Without delay she seated herself on the rug, gave it a crack with her riding-whip, and up rose the rug into the air. It carried her straight to the place where the hunter was living with his wife, the emperor's daughter.

She allowed herself to descend to the ground a short distance from the hunter's dwelling and left her rug and riding-whip lying there. Then she hid among some bushes close to the house entrance and watched until the princess came out for her evening walk. The princess had gone only a little way when the gypsy woman joined her, as if by chance, and they went along together. Presently the gypsy woman artfully induced her companion to turn aside on a bypath that took them to where the magic rug lay outspread on the grass.

No sooner did the princess see it than she exclaimed: "Why, here is a nice rug! Let us sit on it."

Nothing could have pleased the gypsy woman better. They seated themselves on the rug, she gave it a blow with her riding whip, and away they went through the air to the imperial castle as swift as the wind.

The joy of the emperor was boundless when his daughter was restored to him, and he gave the gypsy woman a generous reward. Afterward he shut the princess up in her room and forbade her to leave it.

There she had to stay with two maids to watch and wait on her.

The hunter and his servants were a good deal disconcerted by the disappearance of the princess, and the fox did not rest til he learned what had become of her. Then he summoned his fellow animals to a council and addressed them in these words, "Friends and comrades, we succeeded in marrying our master to the daughter of the emperor, but she has been forcibly taken away, and he is left lonely. We must bring her back. She is now in the imperial castle kept under strict watch, and is never allowed to leave her chamber. It is only by strategy that we can regain possession of her."

"What shall we do?" the bear asked.

"Well," the fox said, "I can think of nothing better than to have the bird of the desert carry me to the emperor's garden. After we get there I will transform myself into a pretty, striped kitten, and will play about under the princess's window. When she sees me she will send her maids to catch me. But I shall not allow myself to be caught until the princess herself comes out. Bird of the Desert, you are to be near at hand, and the moment she seizes me you are to pick her up and carry us both back here."

They all agreed that this was a good plan, and the bird of the desert immediately took the fox on his back and flew with him to the imperial castle. There he set him down. No sooner did Reynard feel solid ground under his feet than he transformed himself into a pretty striped kitten and began to spring about in the most graceful and fantastic fashion beneath the window of the princess's chamber. Thus he succeeded in attracting her attention, and she sent her maids down to bring the kitten to her. But Reynard, though a cat in form, still had a fox's cunning, and he did not allow himself to be caught.

When the princess saw how the kitten eluded her maids she came out herself and joined in the chase, and she caught the kitten with no trouble at all. But that instant the bird of the desert flew forth from his place of concealment, seized her with the kitten still in her grasp, and bore them away to the home of the hunter.

As soon as the emperor was informed of what had happened, he ordered his army to prepare for war and to march as promptly as possible against the hunter and his beasts.

About the time that the army set forth on its expedition Reynard learned of the emperor's plans and summoned his comrades to consider what was to be done.

"We are in great peril," he said. "The emperor is marching with his whole army to exterminate us. Our only way to defeat him is to raise a great force of our friends and make a brave stand against him. Mr. Bear, how many bears can you muster?"

"More than three hundred," the bear replied.

"What can you do, Mr. Wolf?" the fox asked next.

"I can bring five hundred wolves," the wolf answered.

"And you, Bird of the Desert, what help can you furnish?" the fox inquired.

"I promise to recruit at least two hundred birds like myself," was the response.

"Splendid!" the fox cried. "Go, all of you, and assemble your forces. When they are ready I will tell you what to do next."

So the bear and wolf betook themselves to the forest, and the great bird flew off to the desert. Soon heaven and earth resounded with the din of approaching multitudes. Here came the army of bears, there came the wolves, and the sky was darkened as with a thundercloud by the host of birds of the desert.

When the creatures were all drawn up in martial array the fox said: "Tonight, after the emperor has encamped, you bears must go and stampede all his horses. But he will procure fresh horses, and the next night you wolves must creep into the camp and gnaw all the saddles so they will be useless. However, the emperor will get another supply of saddles, and on the third day will be ready to begin his match. As soon as he starts, you birds of the desert must be prepared to drop great pieces of rock down on the army."

All agreed to do as the fox had ordered, and the several detachments of the beasts set forth. The first night, when the imperial host had encamped, the bears drove off all the horses. Early the next morning the soldiers went to the emperor and said, "Wild beasts prowled into the camp last night and frightened the horses so that they have all run away."

"Then get more horses," the emperor commanded, "and be ready to march on the morrow."

The horses were procured, but on the second night the wolves came and gnawed the saddles. In the morning the soldiers awoke and saw the havoc and went to the emperor. "Your Majesty," they said, bending low, "some wild creatures again entered the camp last night, and they have ruined all the saddles by gnawing them to tatters."

"Then buy more saddles and be ready to march to-morrow at dawn," the emperor ordered.

More saddles were hurriedly bought, and the next morning the troops mounted their horses to ride forward on their expedition. But they had scarcely started when the birds of the desert began to let fall great numbers of heavy stones into the midst of the troops. The men became frightened and confused, their horses pranced about in terror, and the emperor shouted: "My brave soldiers, it is impossible for you to fight when you are assailed in such a fashion. Let the hunter and the beasts keep my daughter. I command you to retreat before you are destroyed by the rocks that descend on us from the sky."

So away they all went as fast as they could go, and after that the hunter and his wife lived in peace and joy to the end of their days.

The Hungry Fox
and His Breakfast

Once THERE WAS a fox who lived all alone in a little house in the forest. He woke up one morning and went to the cupboard to get something to eat, and found nothing there.

"Well," he said, "if I am to have any breakfast I shall have to go and look around in the woods for it."

So out he went and rambled along a forest byway until he met a hen. She was afraid of him and flew over to the other side of the road.

"You needn't be scared," the fox said. "I used to eat hens, but I have given up those old ways of mine."

"Where are you going?" the hen asked.

"Oh, I'm just going for a walk," the fox replied. "You can go with me if you like. I will let you ride on my back."

"Thank you," the hen said, "I think I would like to go if I can ride on your back."

"Get on, then," the fox said, "and make yourself comfortable."

So the hen got on his back and the fox walked on. Presently they met a dove, and the dove started to fly away.

"You needn't fly away because you are afraid of me," the fox called out. "I used to eat doves, but I don't anymore."

"Where are you going?" the dove asked.

"I am going for a walk," the fox answered. "Do you see this hen that I have on my back? She is going with me. I am giving her a ride, and I will give you a ride, too."

"That will be very nice," the dove said, "and I will go with you."

She flew to the fox's back and settled down beside the hen. Then the fox resumed his walk, and after a time he met a mouse. As soon as the mouse saw the fox he ran into the tall roadside grass and hid.

"Little mouse," the fox said, "you needn't be frightened. I used to eat little mice, but I don't anymore."

"Where are you going?" the mouse asked.

"I'm going for a walk," the fox replied. "The hen and the dove that you see on my back are going with me. There's room for one more if you care to ride."

"I don't often have a chance to ride," the mouse responded, "and I think I will go."

The fox helped the mouse onto his back and walked on and on by a roundabout way until he reached his home.

"This is where I live," he said to the passengers he was carrying. "Come in and see what a nice little house it is."

He was so polite and had been so kind in giving them a ride that they could not well refuse. But as soon as he had them inside he slammed the door shut and locked it.

Then he turned to the hen and said, "Now I will have my breakfast, and I will begin with you."

"Have mercy!" the hen cried. "Why should you treat me so?"

"You scratch in the garden," the fox said. And he pounced on her and ate her.

"Now, dove, it's your turn," he said.

"Spare me!" the dove begged. "Surely, I have not done anything."

"No!" the fox snorted, "you have not, and that is just the trouble. You are a lazy thing who sits idle on the roof all day and never works."

He made a sudden leap, seized the dove in his sharp teeth and ate her.

Then he looked about once more and said, "Come here, mouse."

But the mouse was not there. He had found a

crack at the bottom of the door and had crawled through it. As soon as he was outside he hastened to the road and ran along it until he met a man with a gun.

"Mr. Man," he said, "a wicked fox lives in a little house back here, and he has just killed and eaten a hen and a dove! He invited them and me into his house, but I crawled out of a crack under the door and ran away. I will show you where he lives."

"Go ahead, then," the man said, "and I will follow you."

Pretty soon they approached the fox's house. Reynard saw them coming, and he jumped out of a window and started to run; but he was not quite quick enough, and the man shot him.

"Ha, ha!" the little mouse laughed, and he climbed up on a stump and waved his tail.

THE HEN, THE DOVE, AND THE MOUSE GO FOR A RIDE

REYNARD AND
THE LITTLE BIRDS

Once UPON A TIME a little bird built a nest in a hedge, laid some eggs in the nest, and hatched a brood of young birds. She was very happy taking care of her family until one day a fox came prowling around and discovered the fledglings. "Aha! Here's a fine breakfast for me," he said to himself. And then he addressed the mother bird who was singing gaily nearby.

"Good-morning, little bird," he said. "How beautiful you are, and how sweetly you sing! But though I admire you and your song, I like better still your young ones in the nest here in the hedge. I intend to eat them."

His words made the little bird feel very anxious, but she concealed her distress and said with a smile, "What! Eat these tiny birds? You are not as clever as I thought if you would do that. They would not make you a mouthful. Wait until they are grown and then return and eat both them and me."

"Good!" the fox exclaimed, "that is just what I will do."

So the bird appointed a day when he was to have his feast, and the fox walked off whistling in high glee.

Not long afterward the bird went to a dog and said, "I know how you can get a delicious meal."

"How?" the dog asked.

The bird told him of her arrangement with the fox, and said in conclusion, "You have only to be on hand when the appointed day comes, and you will catch the fox very easily"

"I will be there," the dog assured her. "This is what I call a stroke of luck. I'll tell you what you must do, little bird. I will hide in the bushes near your nest, and when the fox arrives, you must beg him to delay eating you and your children until you have sung one last song. He surely will not refuse such a request. Then perch on a twig and sing out loud and clear. That will be the signal for me. I will spring from my ambush, and — snap! All will be over with Mr. Fox."

"I shall try to do everything exactly as you have planned," the little bird agreed.

When the appointed day came the fox drew near the hedge where the little bird had her nest, saying to himself,

"These fat little birds, so tender and

> *sweet,*
> *Will make a fine dinner for me to eat."*

Then he saw the mother bird and her young ones sitting on a branch of the hedge. "Well, little bird, how goes it?" he said.

"I have been expecting you," she responded, "and here we are waiting. But before you eat us I have one last request to make — let me sing my favorite song just once more."

"Yes, yes, sing away for all I care," the fox said, "only be quick about it."

So the little bird perched on one of the topmost twigs of the hedge and began her song right lustily. The dog heard her, where he was lurking in a neighboring thicket, and in a twinkling he rushed forth, seized the fox and killed and ate him. So the little bird and her children were rid of their enemy and they lived in the hedge unmolested and happy until the chill of the approaching winter made them fly away to the warm southland.

THE FOX AND HIS FIVE HUNGRY COMRADES

Once UPON A TIME there was a man and his wife who dwelt in a little house far away from any neighbors. But the loneliness of their situation did not trouble them, and they would have been perfectly happy if it had not been for a marten who came nearly every night to their poultry yard and carried off one of their fowls.

The man contrived all sorts of traps to catch the thief, but the marten was clever enough to avoid them. At last, the man stumbled over one of his own traps in the dusk of a winter evening, and he fell and struck his head against a stone and was killed.

Not long afterward the marten came along on the lookout for his supper. He saw the man lying there lifeless, and he said, "Here is a prize. I must see if I can get this man away into the forest before he is found."

A light sledge stood near by, and with great effort the marten got the man onto it and began to drag the sledge toward the forest. He had not gone far when he met a squirrel.

"Good-evening," the squirrel remarked with a bow, "what is that you are dragging behind you?"

The marten laughed and said: "Did you ever hear of anything so strange? I am drawing a sledge with a dead man on it. This man set traps about his hen-house, thinking to catch me. But I was too sly for him, and tonight he stumbled over one of his own traps and was killed. He is very heavy. I wish you would help me draw the sledge."

The squirrel was quite willing to help, and the sledge moved slowly along.

By and by a hare came running across a near field and stopped to find out why the marten and the squirrel were dragging the sledge. "What have you got there?" he asked. And the marten told his story and begged the hare to help pull.

So the hare took hold and pulled his hardest.

After a while a fox joined them, and then a wolf, and lastly a bear. The bear was so large and strong that he was of more use in pulling the sledge than all the other five beasts put together. They went on until they were deep in the forest. Then they ate the man, and for a time their appetite was satisfied. But at length they began to get hungry again, and the wolf, who was the hungriest of all, said, "What shall we eat now, my friends?"

"I suppose we shall have to eat the smallest of us," the bear replied.

"Yes, that is what we will do," the wolf said.

"I quite agree with the bear and the wolf," the fox affirmed.

"So do I," the hare declared.

"Those are my sentiments, too," the marten said. And he turned around to seize the squirrel who was smaller than any of the others. But the squirrel ran up a tree, quick as a flash. Then the marten remembered that he was the next in size, and he hastily slipped into a hole in the rocks.

"What shall we do now?" the wolf asked when he had recovered from his surprise.

"We must eat the smallest of us," the bear said, and stretched out a paw toward the hare.

But the hare darted away into the woods before the bear's paw touched him.'

Now that the squirrel, the marten, and the hare were gone, the fox was the smallest of the three who were left. The wolf and the bear explained that they were very sorry, but they would have to eat him.

Instead of making an attempt to escape, the fox smiled at the other two and remarked, "Things taste stale on the lowlands. Why should you eat here? One's appetite is much better on a mountain."

"You are right," the bear agreed; "and as there is a mountain close at hand, we will climb it before we begin feasting."

They started at once and chose a path that led up the mountainside. The fox trotted cheerfully along with his two big companions, but presently managed to whisper to the wolf, "Tell me what you will have for your next meal after I am eaten."

This question disturbed the wolf very much. What would they have for their next meal, and who would be there to eat it? They had made a rule always to dine off the smallest of the party, and certainly he was smaller than the bear.

These thoughts flashed through his head, and he hastened to say: "Dear brothers, would it not be better for us to live together as comrades than to devour each other? We could hunt and bring in the game and all share it. Is not my plan a good one?"

"Nothing could be better," the fox responded.

The bear would very much have preferred a good dinner at once to any friendship, but the others were two to one, and he had to be content.

For some time all went smoothly, the three companions secured plenty of game and had all they wanted to eat. They got through the winter very well, and then they dissolved their partnership and returned to their homes.

A few weeks later the fox was wandering one morning in the forest when he noticed a magpie's nest in the top branches of a tall, slender tree. He was particularly fond of young magpies, and he considered how he could get one for his dinner. At last he thought of a plan that seemed promising, and he sat down near the tree and began to stare hard at it.

The magpie was watching him from a bough, and she asked, "What are you looking at, Mr. Fox?"

"I'm looking at this tree," he replied. "I intend to make some new snowshoes, and this is just the right tree to cut them out of."

The magpie screeched with alarm when she heard him say that. "Oh, don't use this tree, I implore you, dear brother!" she exclaimed. "I have built my nest in it, and my young ones are not yet old enough to fly."

"It would not be easy to find another tree that would make such good snowshoes," the fox responded, and he cocked his head on one side and gazed at the tree thoughtfully. "But I do not like to be inconsiderate," he continued; "so, if you will give me one of your young ones, I will seek my snowshoes elsewhere."

The magpie did not know what else to do, and she agreed. Then she flew to her nest with a heavy heart and pushed out one of her young ones. The fox seized it in his mouth and ran off in triumph, while the magpie, though deeply grieved for the loss of her little one, found some comfort in the thought that only a bird of extraordinary wisdom would have dreamed of saving the rest by the sacrifice of one.

However, not many days had passed when the fox again came and sat under that same tree and stared at it steadfastly. A dreadful pang shot through the heart of the magpie as she peeped at him from a hole in the nest.

"What are you looking at? " she asked in a trembling voice.

"At this tree," he answered. "I was just thinking what good snowshoes it would make."

"Oh, my dear brother, do go away!" the magpie cried, and she hopped about in anguish. "You know it was only the other day that you promised to get your snowshoes somewhere else."

"So I did," the fox acknowledged, "but though I have searched far and wide I cannot find a single tree that is as good as this. I am sorry to disturb you, but really it is not my fault. The only thing I can do for you is to promise to continue my search for a suitable tree if you will give me another of your young ones."

The poor magpie felt obliged to push a second of her young ones out of the nest, and she had not the consolation now of thinking that she was cleverer than other people.

After the fox left she sat on the edge of her nest, her head drooping and her feathers all ruffled, looking very miserable. Indeed, she was so different from the gay, jaunty magpie, whom every creature in the forest knew, that a crow flying past stopped to find out what the matter was. He looked into the nest and said, "There should be two more young ones in there. Where are they?"

"I had to give them to a fox," the magpie replied. "He has been here twice in the last week, and he was going to cut down my tree to make snowshoes out of it. Each time I had to give him one of my young ones to save the tree."

"Oh, you foolish bird!" the crow cried; "the fox could not have cut down the tree. He has neither axe nor knife. He was only trying to frighten you. Dear me, to think that you have sacrificed your young ones for nothing! Where are your brains?"

Then the crow flew away leaving the magpie overcome with shame and sorrow.

The next morning the fox returned to play his old trick on the magpie, but this time, instead of a cowering, timid bird, he found one with head erect and a determined voice, "You sly fox!" she said, "until you show me the axe or the knife you propose to use in cutting down this tree, you waste words in telling me that you intend to make snowshoes of it."

"Who has been giving you good advice?" the fox asked.

"A crow who visited me yesterday," the magpie replied.

"A crow, was it?" the fox said. "Well, he had better not meet me or it may be the worse for him."

The fox had no desire to continue the conversation with the magpie, and he went away. By and by he came forth from the forest into the open country and stretched himself out in a road just as if he were dead. Very soon he noticed, as he watched from the corner of his eye, that a crow was flying toward him. There he lay stiff and still with his tongue hanging out of his mouth. The crow, who wanted something to eat very badly, alighted near by and hopped along till he was close to the motionless Reynard.

"I wonder if this is the fox the magpie was telling me about," he said. "Well, here the vandal is dead. The fellow has met the fate he deserved quicker than I would have expected."

After looking at him first with one eye and then with the other, the crow stooped forward to peck at his tongue. Instantly the fox gave a snap and caught the intruder by the wing.

The crow knew it was of no use to struggle, and he

said: "Brother Fox, if you are really going to eat me, I beg you at least to do so in good style. Close by is a precipice. Why not first throw me over that so my feathers will be scattered about as I tumble down the rocks? Then all who see them will know that your cunning is greater than mine."

This idea pleased the fox, who had a special grudge against the crow for depriving him of the young magpies. So he carried his captive to the edge of the precipice and threw him over, intending to go around by a path he knew and pick him up at the bottom.

But no sooner was the wily bird released from the fox's jaws than he checked his fall by waving his wings. Then he hovered just out of reach of his enemy and said jeeringly, "Ah, Fox! You know well enough how to catch, but you cannot keep."

The fox turned away and slunk into the forest with his tail between his legs. He did not think now there was much prospect of his catching any game that day, for the crow was sure to fly back ahead of him and put all the animals on their guard.

Presently he met his old friend, the bear. Bruin's wife had died the night before, and he had started out that morning to get some one to mourn over her. He had not gone very far from his comfortable cave when he came across the wolf.

"Where are you going?" the wolf inquired.

"My wife has just died, and I am going to find a mourner," the bear replied.

"Let me mourn for you," the wolf said.

"Do you understand how to howl?" the bear asked.

"Certainly, certainly," the wolf assured him.

"Well, I wish you would favor me with a specimen of your howling to make sure that you know your business," the bear said.

So the wolf broke forth in a song of lament. "Hu, hu, hu, hum, hoh!" he shouted, and he made such a noise that the bear put his paws up to his ears and begged him to stop.

"You have no idea how to do it," the bear growled angrily. "Be off with you."

A little farther on the hare was resting in a ditch. He saw the bear and came out and spoke to him. "Why do you look so sad?" he inquired.

"My wife has died," the bear answered, "and I am searching for a mourner who can lament over her properly."

"I will gladly do the lamenting for you," the hare said.

"Before I accept your kind offer," the bear responded, "I would like to have you give me a proof of your talents."

"Pu, pu, pu, pum, poh!" the hare piped. But he had

such a weak, small voice that the bear could hardly hear him .

"No, that is not what I want," the bear said. "I will bid you good-morning."

Later in the day he met the fox, and the fox also observed the bear's altered looks and stopped to speak with him. "What is the matter with you?" the fox asked.

"My wife has died, and I am seeking for a mourner," the bear answered.

"I will do the mourning," the fox said.

Bruin looked at him thoughtfully. "Can you howl well?" he questioned.

"Yes, beautifully," the fox declared. "Just listen." And he lifted up his voice and cried: "Loo, loo, loo! Mrs. Bear, the famous spinner, the baker of toothsome cakes, the prudent housekeeper, is torn from her husband! Loo, loo, loo! She is gone, she is gone!"

"Now at last I have found some one who understands the art of lamentation," the bear exclaimed with a grunt of satisfaction. "Come with me to my cave."

So he led the way to his cave and showed the fox the body of Mrs. Bear lying on a bed of moss. There he left Reynard to mourn while he went outside and started a fire that he might cook some soup for the mourner.

Presently the bear bethought himself that he did

not hear any of the howling lamentation he was expecting. Ladle in hand, he entered the cave and there,
to his horror, he found the fox eating the dead bear,
instead of wailing over her. The fox dashed out of the
door, and the bear threw his ladle at him. But the fox
escaped unhurt. That ended whatever friendship had
existed between the bear and the fox, and they never
had anything to do with each other afterward.

THE FIVE HUNGRY BEASTS DRAWING
THE SLEDGE TO THE FOREST

THE CRAFTY FOX AND THE INDUSTRIOUS GOOSE

Once THERE WAS a fox and a goose who were close friends, and for a time they got along very well together in spite of the fact that the fox was crafty and lazy and the goose honest and industrious.

One day the goose said to the fox, "Friend Fox, I have a piece of land, and if you will help me, we will cultivate it and raise some wheat to eat next winter."

"I would be greatly pleased to join with you in this enterprise," the fox said.

"We will do all the necessary work together, share and share alike," the goose told him.

"Very well," the fox agreed.

They met shortly afterward, and the goose said, "It is time to plough our land."

"Yes, I think it is," the fox responded, "but that is none of my business. You will have to do the ploughing."

So the goose did the ploughing, and then she went

to the fox and said, "It is time to sow the seed."

"You are quite right," the fox said, "and the quicker the sowing is done the better. But that is your business. I have nothing to do with it myself."

So the goose did the sowing. Some months later she said to the fox, "Friend, the grass is choking the wheat. We must pull it out."

"Certainly, it ought to be pulled out," the fox remarked with a wise nod of his head, "and you had better do the pulling as soon as possible. That is not my business."

So the goose pulled the grass out. By and by the wheat was ripe, and the goose said to the fox, "Our wheat must be reaped."

"Alright," the fox said, "you attend to that. It is not my business."

So the goose reaped the wheat. A few days afterward she sought the fox and said, "It is time to put our wheat in the barn and do the threshing."

"Well, then," the fox said, "I advise you to hustle and get it in before we have rain. After it is in the barn go right at the threshing. Those things are none of my business. You must attend to them yourself. Let me know when the work is done and I will go to the barn and see what sort of a crop we have raised."

The goose got the wheat in and threshed it. But she had begun to feel distrustful of her friend, the fox.

He had been sauntering about the forest all the months that she had been so busy with the wheat and had not helped her in the least. "I think I will consult the greyhound," she said to herself. "He is a shrewd fellow whose advice would be worth having."

She soon found the greyhound, and when he heard her story he said: "The fox has been playing tricks on your good nature right along, and no doubt he will do so again if he has the chance. Take me to the barn before you tell him that the wheat is threshed and hide me in the sheaves so that only one of my eyes will be uncovered. I want to see what happens when he comes, but I don't want him to know that I am there."

The goose went to the barn with* the greyhound, and after she had him hid she brought the fox. Reynard was much delighted to see all the nice clean straw and the great heap of splendid grain. He began to dance about and sing: —

"Hurrah, hurrah!
Both straw and wheat are mine!
Hurrah, hurrah!
Both straw and wheat are mine!"

While he was singing he approached the place where the greyhound was hiding in the straw, and saw his eye.

"Ah, there's a grape!" he cried.

"But it is not ripe!" the greyhound shouted, and he leaped out of his hiding place and killed the crafty fox.

So the goose had all the straw and wheat, and she fared very comfortably that winter.

THE FOX AND THE WICKED WOLF

Once A WOLF AND A fox lived together in the same den. But the wolf treated the fox very roughly, and one day the fox said to him: "Be not so unkind to me, I pray you. If you persist in ill-using me, punishment will surely overtake you sooner or later."

This appeal made the wolf angry, and he gave the fox a blow that knocked him down, senseless. But after a while the fox recovered and said to the wolf: "I crave your pardon for my fault-finding. In future I hope to avoid displeasing you."

"I will forgive you only on condition that you promise to be my slave," the wolf responded. "You know very well now how severe I can be to those who offend me."

The fox prostrated himself before the wolf and said, "I will be your slave, and may you live long and never fail to subdue those who oppose you."

After that the fox bore the wolf's insolence and abuse in silence, but he was far from being contented. One day, as he was rambling about, he noticed a break in the wall of a vineyard.

"Here is a chance to slip through and get some grapes," he said. "But caution is the half of cleverness—perhaps this break in the wall has been made to deceive and ensnare me."

He went nearer and examined the gap warily; and lo! Just the other side of it was a deep pit which the vineyard people had dug. The pit had a slight covering to conceal it and was well arranged to catch in it any wild beast that came through the gap to despoil the vines.

The fox drew back from it, exclaiming: "Heaven be praised that I looked about instead of leaping through the gap in my haste to get some grapes! I hope that my cruel master, the wolf, will fall into this pit and perish so I shall be freed from my servitude."

He laughed and shook his head and hurried off to find the wolf. As soon as he caught sight of him, he said: "You have often observed that vineyard which the beasts all have such difficulty to get into on account of the stout and high wall which surrounds it. I have just come from there to tell you that there is a breach in the wall through which you might easily slip."

"You must lose no time in guiding me to the spot," the wolf commanded.

They trotted away together, and when they came to a gap in the wall the wolf bolted through. Down he went through the covering of the pit, and the fox exclaimed joyfully: "Now has fortune favored me! My wicked master will trouble me no more."

He crept to the edge of the pit and looked down. There was the wolf weeping in sorrow for himself, and the fox wept, too.

The wolf looked up and asked, "Do you weep because of your compassion for me?"

"No," the fox answered, "I weep for the length of your past life and in regret at your not having been caught in some trap or pit sooner. If you had been snared and killed before I met you, I would have had much more of ease and comfort."

"You evil-minded fox!" the wolf said; "go to my mother and tell her what has happened to me. Perhaps she can contrive some way of getting me out of here."

"Not so," the fox responded. "You have been entrapped by the excess of your covetousness and have fallen into a pit from which you will never be saved."

"O Fox," the wolf said, "you have up until now feared the greatness of my power and always manifested an affection for me and a desire for my friendship. Do not now be angry with me for my treatment of you. Forgive my offenses and show me kindness. Can you not find some means of delivering me from destruction?"

"You artful, wicked, treacherous wolf!" the fox said, "Hope not for deliverance. You are going to be justly punished for your base conduct. As you have sown so shall you reap."

"O gentlest of the beasts of prey," the wolf resumed, "you surely are more faithful than to leave me in this pit. I have always found you ready to aid me in the past."

"Stupid enemy! " the fox exclaimed, "how are you reduced to humility and submission after your tyranny and haughtiness! I kept company with you through fear of your oppression, and flattered you with the hope of winning your favor."

"Speak not with hostility," the wolf entreated. "Go and get a rope and tie one end to a tree and let the other end down to me. Then I will lay hold of it and escape from this horrid spot. Do as I bid you and I will give you all the treasures that I possess."

"No," the fox said, "you will never escape through my help. Reflect on your wickedness and the cruel way you treated me. Know that your soul is about to quit this world and go to an evil abode where you should have been long before."

It was plain to the wolf that the fox had no kindly feeling for him, and he said, "I have been careless in the past, but if I am delivered from this affliction, I will surely repent of my overbearing conduct to those who are weaker than I."

He wept and lamented until the heart of the fox was moved with tenderness for him. Then the fox placed himself at the brink of the pit and sat so that his tail hung down in the cavity. Immediately the wolf reached up with his front paws, caught hold of the fox's tail, and attempted to pull himself out of the pit, but he pulled with such haste and violence that the fox lost his footing and tumbled down beside him.

"Now you have become my companion," the wolf said, "and you are in my power. Why did you rejoice in my misfortune? Punishment has quickly overtaken you. I will hasten your slaughter that you may not behold mine."

"Delay your vengeance," the fox begged, "for I have a plan that may get us both out of this pit."

"O you wily deceiver!" the wolf said; "I do not trust you, but tell me your plan."

"It is one for which you ought to reward me generously," the fox responded. "When I heard your promises, and your confession of past misconduct, and your regrets at not having repented and done good, I felt sorry for you and hung my tail down into the pit.

But with your usual habit of haste and violence you pulled me in such a way that I thought my soul had departed. I slipped back over the edge and became your companion in this place of destruction and death. My plan is the only possibility of release."

"Well," the wolf said, "and what is it you have to propose?"

The fox answered: "I would have you stand upright and allow me to climb onto your shoulders. Then I can reach up to the edge of the pit and pull myself out. Afterward I will go and bring something that you can take hold of and deliver yourself with."

"I put no confidence in your words," the wolf commented, "but it is my only chance to get out of here. So I accept your proposal." The wolf raised himself upright, and the fox got on his shoulders and sprang up to the surface.

"O my friend!" the wolf called, "Do not forget me nor delay my deliverance."

The fox uttered a loud laugh and said: "You are my enemy. Never again will I put myself in your power."

"Verily," the wolf said softly, "you foxes are the sweetest of people in tongue and the most pleasant in jesting. But not every time is appropriate for sport and joking."

"O idiot!" the fox responded, "You seek deliverance in vain. Your fate is sealed." He then went to a mound that overlooked the vineyard and called to some men working among the vines. They saw him and ran toward him and he hastened to escape through the gap in the wall.

The men came to the pit, and there they saw the wolf and stopped. Then they picked up heavy stones and pelted the captive and killed him. After that the fox dwelt in security in the den where he and the wolf had lived together, and for all that I know, there he dwells still.

The Fox Who Became A Shepherd

There WAS ONCE an old woman who went to market and bought some sheep. She drove them home and put them in the barn and said: "Now I must get a shepherd. The sheep will have to be turned out to graze, and a shepherd must be with them to take care of them."

So early the next day she started out to look for a shepherd. On and on she walked over the hills until she met a bear.

"Good-morning," the bear said; "where are you going today?"

"I am looking for some one to watch my sheep," she told him.

"Hire me," the bear said. "I'll watch them."

"Your voice is rather gruff," the old woman responded. "Can you talk softly to them?"

"Yes," the bear answered. "This is the way I will

call them — Gr-r-r! Gr-r-r! Gr-r-r!"

"Oh, no!" the old woman exclaimed, and stopped her ears. "Such a call as that would scare the wits out of them. They would run away."

So she left the bear and walked on and on until she met a wolf.

"Good-morning," the wolf said; "where are you going today?"

"I am looking for some one to watch my sheep," she replied.

"I can watch them," the wolf told her. "Hire me."

"But I'm not sure about that voice of yours," she said. "Could you talk softly to my sheep?"

"Yes," the wolf declared; "I will call them like this—Wow ! Wow!"

"No, no!" the old woman cried; "I could not have a shepherd who called them in that rude tone. They would run away."

So she left the wolf and walked on and on until she met a fox.

"Good-morning," the fox said; "where are you going today?"

"I am looking for some one to watch my sheep," she told him.

"That is just the job for me," the fox asserted.

"Well," the old woman said, "you have a pleasant voice. I think perhaps you will do, but I should want to be very sure that you could talk softly to my sheep."

"Oh, I would do that!" the fox promised. "This is the way I would call them — Ooo! Ooo! Ooo!"

"Very good," the old woman said. "I will hire you."

The fox went home with her, and she let the sheep out of the barn and told him to take care of them while they were grazing.

Night came, and the cunning fox brought the sheep safely home, but the next night one of them was missing.

"They are not all here," the old woman said. "Where is the missing one?"

"The wolf ate it," the fox replied. "He came out of the woods while I was not looking and carried it off before I could stop him."

"You must be more careful after this," the old woman cautioned him.

But the very next night another sheep was gone, and the old woman asked the fox where it was.

"The bear ate it," the fox answered. "He came from behind a rock while I was not looking and carried the sheep off before I could stop him."

"You must keep on the lookout all the time," the old woman ordered. "Unless you can do better, I shall have to turn you off and hire another shepherd."

The next morning, soon after the fox had driven the sheep out to where they were to graze, the old woman filled a bowl with milk and said, "I will carry this to my shepherd." She walked along with her cane in one hand and the bowl of milk in the other. Presently she climbed a little hill, and there was the fox in a hollow before her standing over a dead sheep. She looked at his bloody jaws and knew it was he who had killed the other two sheep as well as that one.

"You wretch!" the old woman cried. "You robber! You villain!"

She strode toward him threateningly. The fox did not like the look of her stout cane, and he started to run. Then the old woman in her wrath threw the bowl of milk at him. It struck the end of his tail, and from that day to this the tail of the fox has had a white tip.

THE OLD WOMAN THROWS THE MILK AT THE FOX

The Fox, the Wolf, and the Cheese

At THE FOOT of some high mountains there was once a small village with a road entering it from the east, and this road was joined by one from the south on the village borders. One summer night, when a round, full moon was shining, a wolf came trotting along the eastern road.

"I must get a good meal before I go back to my den in the mountains," he said to himself. "It is nearly a week since I have tasted anything but scraps. There are plenty of rabbits and hares in the forest, but they are so swift I would need to be a greyhound to catch them, and I am not as young as I was. I wish I could dine on that lady fox I saw a fortnight ago. I would have caught and eaten her right then, but her husband was nearby, and I did not want to fight two such active, sharp-toothed creatures. Well, I am going to see what I can pick up in this village."

While the wolf was talking thus to himself, the very fox that he so desired to eat was coming along the southern road, and she was saying, "The whole of this day I have listened to the clucking of those village hens till I can keep away no longer. It is the sweetest of all music when one is fond of fowls and eggs. As sure as I live I will have some of those hens this night."

Just then she reached a little plot of grass where the two roads joined, and she lay down there under a tree to rest. Soon afterward the wolf came along and saw her, and she turned her head at the sound of his footfalls and saw him. It was too late for her to escape, and she suppressed her fear and made a pretense at friendliness.

"Is that you, neighbor?" she said politely. "I hope you are well."

"I am as well as any one can be who is very hungry," the wolf said, and his eyes glistened greedily. "But what is the matter with you? A fortnight ago you were as plump as heart could wish."

"I have been sick," the fox explained, " and am so thin that my very bones rattle."

"But you are still good enough for me," the wolf said, and he started toward her with open mouth.

"What are you doing?" the fox cried, stepping backward.

"What am I doing!" the wolf retorted. "I'm going after my supper, and I shall eat you in less time than a rooster takes to crow."

"Oh, you are always joking!" she remarked anxiously, never removing her eyes from the wolf.

"I am too hungry to waste time joking," the wolf said with a snarl that showed all his teeth. "I want to eat you — not to talk to you."

"Remember that I have children at home," the fox said. "Pity a poor mother." And she wiped her eyes with the tip of her tail.

But the wolf showed plainly that her appeal did not move him, and that his patience was about exhausted. So she hastened to ask him to grant one last request.

"What is it?" the wolf growled.

"In this village there is an old well," the fox responded, "and its owner stores cheeses in it. Two buckets hang from a pole above it, and I come frequently and descend in one of the buckets into the well and bring away with me enough cheese to feed my children. My request is that you let me go and make one more good meal off the cheese before I die."

"I'd rather like some cheese myself," the wolf said. "Lead the way and we will go to the well." •

So they went on together, but as they were creeping softly into the village the fox made a sudden leap over a wall hoping to elude her companion. However, he sprang over after her and was instantly at her side. "I think I had better curb your desire to jump by taking a bite out of your haunch," he said with a menacing snap of his teeth.

The fox drew back uneasily. "Be careful, or I shall scream," she told him.

That would rouse the village, and the wolf had no desire to have her carry out her threat.

Presently they entered a courtyard, and there was the well. The fox looked down into it and saw the reflection of the moon, big, round, and yellow, in the water at the bottom.

"How lucky!" she said to the wolf. "A huge cheese the size of a grindstone lies down there. Look! Look! Did you ever see anything so beautiful?"

"Never," the wolf answered as he peered hungrily into the well.

"You have only to go down in one of these buckets to eat your fill," the fox informed him. "I will wait my turn here."

"Oh, that is your game!" the wolf said with a grin. "No, you can't escape me by any such trick. You must go down yourself and bring the cheese up."

There was nothing the fox could do but obey, and she climbed into the bucket. Down she went to the bottom of the well, and at the same time a bucket on the other end of the rope went up. The bucket in which the fox descended hit the water with a splash, but did not fill, for the well was nearly dry.

"The cheese is even larger and richer than thought," the fox called to the wolf.

"Then hasten and bring it up," the wolf ordered.

"But it is so heavy that I can't," the fox said. "You will have to come down, and then we will carry it up between us."

"And how am I to come down?" the wolf asked.

"Get into that other bucket which is right over your head," the fox replied.

So the wolf with some difficulty climbed into the bucket. He weighed at least four times as much as the fox, and he went down with a jerk, and his weight sent her to the surface with equal rapidity.

As soon as he understood what had happened, he upbraided the fox very angrily. She had leaped out of the bucket and was now looking down at him, "Good-bye," she said sweetly; "I hope you will enjoy the cheese."

Then she went off to a neighboring henhouse where she secured several fat chickens. As she was on her way home she said to herself: "I wonder how Mr. Wolf is getting along. I'm afraid I left him in a bad plight, but I see that the sky has clouded over. If there should be a heavy rain, the other bucket will fill and sink to the bottom of the well and his bucket will go up — at least it may."

HOW THE CAT OUTWITTED THE FOX

ONCE UPON A TIME a cat and a rooster agreed to live together. So they built themselves a hut, and the rooster did the housekeeping while the cat skirmished around and got food for them. Every day, when the cat left the hut, he said to the rooster, "Lock the door as soon as I go out and don't let any one in until I come back." One day, while the cat was away hunting, a fox came rapping at the door of the hut. "Little rooster," he cried, "let me in!"

"Pussy told me not to," the rooster responded.

Again the fox rapped. "Open the door," he shouted.

"I tell you Pussy ordered me not to," the rooster said.

But the fox kept asking to be let in, and at last the rooster grew tired of always saying, "No," and opened the door. In rushed the fox, seized the rooster in his jaws, and ran off with him.

Then the rooster called: —

"O Pussy, dear,
The fox is here!
He holds me tight —
I'm faint from fright!
Unless you 're quick
My bones he'll pick!"

The cat heard the rooster calling, and he chased the fox till he overtook him. Then he made the fox release the rooster, and the two friends went home. On the way Puss gave the rooster some good advice, and said in conclusion, "Now, keep out of that fox's jaws in future, if you don't want to be killed altogether."

Another day, when the cat was out foraging so that he and the rooster might have something to eat, the sly fox again came rapping at the door. "Dear little rooster," the fox said, "pray let me in."

"No, Mr. Fox," the rooster responded, "Pussy told me to keep the door shut and locked."

But the fox kept on asking and asking till at last the rooster let him in. Then the fox rushed at the rooster, seized him by the neck, and ran off with him.

At once the rooster cried out: —

"O Pussy, dear,
The fox is here!
He holds me tight —

I 'm faint from fright!
Unless you're quick
*My bones he'll pick!'**

The rooster's call was heard by the cat, who ran after the fox and compelled him to let his captive go and gave him a sound drubbing. On the way home the cat scolded the rooster roundly and told him never on any plea to let the fox in again. "He is no friend of ours," the cat declared. "All he wants is to eat you."

Not long afterward the fox came once more to the hut when the cat was out hunting for food. "Dear little rooster," he said, "open the door."

"No, Mr. Fox, Pussy told me I wasn't to do so," was the rooster's response.

But the fox begged and begged so persistently that at last the rooster opened the door. Instantly the fox caught the rooster by the throat and ran off with him, and the rooster shouted: —

"O Pussy, dear,
The fox is here!
He holds me tight —
I'm faint from fright,
Unless you 're quick
My bones he'll pick!"

The cat heard the rooster calling and gave chase. He ran and he ran, but this time he could not catch the fox, and he returned home and wept bitterly because now he was all alone. At length, however, he took his fiddle and a big sack and went to the fox's hole. He sat down near it and began to play and sing: —

> *"Fiddle-de-dee,*
> *Fox, listen to me!*
> *Four daughters have you,*
> *A little son, too.*
> *So fiddle-de-dee,*
> *All come out and see*
> *Who fiddles here for you."*

The fox's oldest daughter said to her father: "Daddy, that fiddler plays very nicely. I'm going to see who he is."

Out she skipped, but Pussy was watching, and the moment she appeared he caught her and popped her into his sack. Again he played and sang: —

> *"Fiddle-de-dee,*
> *Fox, listen to me!*
> *Four daughters have you,*
> *A little son, too.*
> *So fiddle-de-dee,*
> *All come out and see*
> *Who fiddles here for you."*

Then the second oldest daughter of the fox skipped out. Pussy caught her and popped her into his sack, and he continued his fiddling and singing until he had caught all four daughters and the little son, too.

The old fox was now left alone. He waited and waited for his children to return, but they did not come. At last he said to himself: "I will go out and call them in, for the rooster is roasted, the soup is ready, and the porridge is on the table. It is high time we had something to eat."

So out he went, and the cat grabbed him and shoved him into the sack with his children. Then the cat went down into the fox's hole and drank all the soup and gobbled up all the porridge. He looked about for something more to eat and saw the roasted rooster lying on a platter beside the fire.

"Come, shake yourself, rooster," Puss said.

So the rooster shook himself and got up, and he and the cat went home together. They carried the sack along, and when winter came they had some nice fox skins on their beds to keep them warm. None of their wild neighbors ever troubled them again, and they lived in their little hut in peace and plenty for the rest of their days.

THE FOX, THE BEAR, AND THE POOR FARMER

Once UPON A TIME there was a farmer who was so poor that he did not own any horses or oxen, and he had to do his ploughing with two cows. One morning he was ploughing in a field that bordered the forest when he heard among the trees a great noise of rustling and crackling and of growling and squeaking.

He left his plough in the furrow, crept softly into the woods, and peered cautiously through the thick underbrush. There he saw a huge bear wrestling with a little rabbit, and the sight of two such ill-matched creatures contending seemed to him so funny that he laughed loud and long.

The bear heard his laughter and was very angry. He let go his hold on the rabbit and strode toward the farmer growling savagely.

"What do you mean by laughing so at me?" he asked.

The poor farmer was now as much frightened as he had been amused a moment before. He could not answer a word.

"I'll teach you not to laugh at me again," the bear snarled. "I'm going to eat you and your two cows."

The bear was rushing at the farmer with wide-open jaws when the trembling man found his tongue. "Oh, please, Mr. Bear," he cried in terror, "I couldn't help laughing! I really couldn't! I beg you not to eat me. I will never, never laugh at you again."

"No, you will not laugh at me again," the bear said. "You won't have the chance. I am going to eat you right now."

The farmer fell on his knees and with tears in his eyes besought the bear to spare him. But the more piteously he entreated, the more fiercely the beast declared that he should be eaten.

Finally the farmer said: "I see I can expect no mercy from you, and I will only ask the privilege of living until evening. Let me have the rest of this day, I beseech you, Mr. Bear, so that I can plough and sow this field. Then my family will not be without bread to eat when winter comes."

To this proposal the bear gave a sullen consent. Then he shambled off and was soon lost to sight in the forest, and the farmer returned to his ploughing.

About noon a fox who was passing that way

stopped to speak to the man. "Why are you looking so sad?" the fox inquired.

"I surely have reason enough to be sad," the farmer answered. "This morning I heard a great racket near by in the woods, and when I went to discover the cause of the noise I found a bear wrestling with a rabbit. I could not help laughing, and that made the bear so angry he was going to eat me at once. I begged for mercy, but he would only grant me the rest of the day, and he is coming back here this very evening to eat me and my two cows."

"If that is all you are mourning about, you need grieve no longer," the fox said cheerfully. "I can tell you how to save your own life and the lives of your two cows as well; and you shall have the skin of that bear for a warm rug in your house."

"But how can such a miracle be done, Mr. Fox?" the farmer asked.

"What will you give me if I tell you? " the fox asked.

At first the farmer did not know what to offer, but presently he agreed to give the fox nine hens and a rooster.

"Very well," the fox said. "Now listen and do just as I tell you. When the bear returns this evening I will be hiding in the bushes. I will make a blowing sound just such as the hunters make when they blow their horns. The bear will ask you,'What is that?'

"You must answer, 'The hunters are coming.'

"The bear will be frightened and beg you to conceal him. I see you have a big sack here in which you brought your seed. Tell the bear to crawl into that and not to stir. Then I will come out of the bushes and ask, 'What is in that sack?'

"You will reply, 'Some sticks of wood.'

"I will not believe you and will say, 'Hit the sack with your axe.'

"You must then seize your axe and strike a mighty blow into the bear's head that will kill him at once."

The farmer was pleased with this advice, and he agreed to follow it. Everything happened as the fox had arranged, and the farmer and his cows were saved.

"Did I not tell you I would rescue you?" the fox said. "Learn from this, my friend, that wit is better than strength. I shall come to your house tomorrow morning for those nine hens and that rooster. Pick out the fattest fowls in your flock, and take care that you are at home, or you will be sorry!"

The farmer loaded the bear on his wagon, hitched his cows to it, and drove joyfully home. Then he ate a hearty supper, went to bed, and slept soundly.

Very early the next morning, when the farmer had scarcely opened his eyes, the fox knocked at the door. "I want that rooster and the nine hens!" he shouted.

"Right away, Brother Fox, right away," the farmer responded. "Just give me time to dress."

But it happened that he had two dogs who were in the habit of staying in the house at night, and they went sniffing at the door and got a scent of the fox. Immediately they began to bark, "Bow-wow-wow! "

"Hello, farmer!" the fox cried anxiously, "what's that I hear? You haven't a hound in there, have you?"

"Yes, two of them," the farmer answered. "They sleep under my bed, and now they have scented you and are trying to get out. I can hardly hold them."

"Oh, Mr. Farmer, don't let them go!" the fox exclaimed. "Hang on to them till I get away from here. Never mind the nine hens and the rooster. You can keep them."

When the farmer opened the door the fox was disappearing over the ridge of a neighboring mountain. The farmer laughed heartily, and if he's still alive he may be laughing yet.

THE BEAR GOES INTO THE FARMER'S SACK

The Proud Fox and the Young Prairie Chicken

One TIME there was a proud fox who was trotting along the road soon after sunrise on a summer's day when he overtook a prairie chicken. The prairie chicken looked very young and simple, and the fox thought that here was a good chance to secure a nice tender morsel for his breakfast.

"Good-morning," he said, and tried to get up close to her.

"Good-morning, yourself," the prairie chicken responded, sidling away from him.

"How are all your folks?" the fox asked.

"They're well[3]," the prairie chicken answered. "How are yours?"

"Oh, fine!" the fox replied.

"I'm glad to hear that," the prairie chicken said. "I

---

[3] Originally "just middling" which literally means "just well" or "fair".

don't know that I've ever seen them, or you either, before. What have you been doing since plant-ing-time?"

"Just running around and enjoying myself when I wasn't learning all that my daddy knows," the fox told her.

"Surely, you don't claim to know all that your daddy has been finding out since he was turned loose on the world," the prairie chicken said.

"Yes, I do," the fox declared. "If there's a slyer fox in these parts than I am, I agree to pin back his ears and swallow him without sauce or seasoning."

"For gracious sake!" the prairie chicken exclaimed.

"I'm telling you the truth," the fox said. "When it comes to slyness I don't take a back seat for any one. Well, and what have you been doing your own self?"

"Nothing in particular," the prairie chicken an-swered, and she hung down her head and looked as ashamed as if all her tail feathers were pulled out. "Ever since I left the egg I have been busy running after my mammy and getting the bugs and seeds she finds. I haven't had time to learn anything except how to hide if I see a man with a gun, or a beast with a hungry-looking tooth showing."

That last remark disturbed the fox some, for he had a hungry tooth himself. He hoped she had not noticed it, and he hastened to turn her thoughts in another direction.

"So you know just one way to hide?" he said. " I've got dozens of ways. Good Lord! Icould tell you ways of hiding from now till sundown. But what is your own little way?"

The prairie chicken was quite overcome with the learning of the fox, and she replied hesitatingly: "I just get underneath the dead leaves. Of course a part of me often sticks out, but that doesn't matter because my feathers and the leaves are exactly the same color."

"I call that a pretty poor way of hiding," the fox remarked.

"Yes," the prairie chicken agreed rather testily, "but it will do me until I can fly. Then I won't need any tricks at all."

The fox was starting to make another brag when some hounds came into sight. At once the prairie chicken caught up a dead leaf and rolled with it just as if the wind were blowing her along. She got out of the path and in among the grass and brush.

So she escaped, but the hounds caught the fox, and his brush now hangs above the chimney-piece of the man who owned the hounds. The brush was all that the hounds left of him.

HOW THE FOX AND THE CRAB RAN A RACE

Once UPON A TIME a fox was walking on the seashore and met a crab. "Crawling thing," the fox said, "did you ever run in your life?"

"Yes," the crab replied, "I very often run from the mud here to the grass yonder and from the grass back to the water."

"Oh, fie!" the fox exclaimed, "That is no distance to run. How many legs have you? "

"Eight," the crab answered.

"Why, if I had as many legs as you have," the fox said, "I could run like the wind. You are really a very slow, stupid creature. It is ridiculous that a person with a whole row of legs along each side should run so slowly."

"Well," the crab said, "I challenge you to run a race if you are not above matching yourself against a dull-witted, sluggish animal like me? But I am much smaller than you are. Suppose we go and weigh ourselves. If you are ten times heavier than I am, of course you ought to run more than ten times faster to win the race. However, never mind about the weight. I know you are swift, but that is just because you have such a fine tail and hold it so high. If you would allow me to fasten something to your tail so it would stay down I think you could not run any faster than I, even if you do weigh so much more."

"Have done with your talking," the fox snorted contemptuously. "Do as you like, for whether my tail is up or down I have no doubt that I shall beat you without any effort at all. Your many legs and your stupid head do not go very well together. If I had your legs and my own sense, not a creature on earth could outrun me. As it is there are none that can outwit me. Even among mankind, such is my reputation that they have a saying, 'As sly as a fox.' So do what you choose, stupid one."

"All I ask," the crab said, "is to fix your beautiful tail so it will stay down. Then I shall surely win the race."

"Oh, no, you will not," the fox retorted. "You can fasten my tail down, but, just the same, I shall prove to your dull brain that you never had the least chance to win. How do you wish that I should hold my tail for you to make sure it will stay down?"

"Just lower it so I can hang something on it," the

crab said.

"Alright," the fox agreed; "only don't keep me standing here all day."

"I shall not be long," the crab promised; "and as soon as I have finished I will call, 'Ready!' Then you are to start."

The crab crawled behind the fox, caught Reynard's bushy tail with his pincers and shouted, "Ready!"

Away sped the fox, and he ran and ran till he was tired. But when he stopped, the crab, who had all the time clung to his tail, was there right beside him.

"What's the matter with you?" the crab asked. "I thought you said you could run ten times faster than I. You are not even ahead of me."

The fox panted for breath and hung his head in shame.

"I feel as fresh as if I had not run at all," the crab declared. "Let's race back in the same way to where we started."

"No," the fox said, "I don't care to do anymore racing with eight-legged people." And he went away into the forest hoping he never would see the crab again.

THE FOX WITH A SACKFUL OF TRICKS

Once UPON A TIME it happened that a cat was searching for mice in the woodland when she saw a fox coming toward her.

"I must speak to him/' she said to herself, "and I had better greet him very politely. He is clever, and he is experienced in all the ways of the world. It will be well to keep on as friendly terms as possible with him."

"Good-morning, dear Mr. Fox," she said. "How do you do, and how are you getting along in these hard times?"

The fox, full of pride, looked at the cat for some time, undecided whether he would deign to answer or not. At last he said: "O you poor whisker-wiper! You piebald simpleton! You starveling mouse-hunter! What has put it in your head to ask me how I am getting on? I wonder that you dare to do it."

"I meant no offense," the cat responded. "You are wise and I am simple. I am slow in thought while your wits are keen and quick. I only venture to go a short distance from home, and so have not your opportunities to acquire knowledge, for your travels take you far and wide. Let us be friends, and I beseech you to share with me some of your wisdom."

"Pooh, pooh!" the fox sneered; "share my wisdom with a foolish cat! However, I am not selfish, and I don't mind telling you a thing or two that you perhaps may find of value sooner or later."

"Thank you," the cat said; "I shall treasure whatever you see fit to tell me."

"Well, then," the fox continued, "what sort of education have you had? How many arts do you understand?"

"Only one," the cat replied meekly.

"And what might that be?" the fox inquired.

"I am almost ashamed to tell you, it is such a poor little art," the cat said.

"I don't doubt it is poor enough," the fox observed with a scornful sniff. "Nevertheless, I would like to hear what it is."

"Why, if you really want to know," the cat said hesitatingly, "the art is one for escaping the dogs. When they run after me I can climb a tree and save myself."

"Is that all you can do?" the fox said, and he

snorted contemptuously. "As for me, I am master of a hundred arts, and I have a sackful of cunning tricks also. Truly, I pity you. Come with me and I will teach you how to escape the dogs without any laborious tree climbing."

Just then a huntsman came riding along accompanied by four hounds. The cat was too frightened to wait for the fox to give her wise advice, and she ran nimbly up a tree.

Nor did she stop until she had perched herself on the topmost bough where she was completely hidden by the twigs and leaves.

The fox remained on the ground down below, and she called to him: "Mr. Fox, open your sackful of tricks! Open it quick or those fierce hounds will catch you."

But while she was speaking the hounds seized poor Reynard, and they held him tight. "O Mr. Fox," the cat said, "you are caught in spite of your hundred arts and sackful of tricks, while I with my one art am safe. Had you been able to climb up here your life would not be forfeited."

REYNARD AND

HIS ADVENTURES

ONCE UPON A TIME a fox lay peeping out of his hole on a winter's morning. There was a road in sight not far away, and by and by he saw a man coming along on it, driving to market with a load of fish.

"That reminds me I haven't had breakfast," the fox said. "Some of the fish on that sledge would just suit me. I think I can play a trick that will make the man give me a chance to help myself to them."

Then he ran down a convenient hollow that allowed him to get into the road some distance ahead of the sledge without being seen, and there he stretched himself motionless by the roadside. Pretty soon the sledge reached him, and the driver pulled up sharply. "Aha, a dead fox!" he said, and he jumped out and tossed Reynard onto his load.

The man got back on his seat and drove on. And soon the fox cautiously wriggled to the rear end of the sledge, threw off two nice large fish, and jumped off himself. Then he took the fish in his mouth and trotted away to the forest. There he met a bear who stopped and asked, "Where did you get those fish, Mr. Fox?"

"Oh! Not far off," the fox answered. "You know the stream in the glen where the elves dwell. I just stuck my tail through a hole in the ice there, and these fish caught on and I pulled them out."

The bear in those days had as long and as fine a tail as the fox, and he said, "Well, if those fish would hang on to your tail, I suppose some would hang on to mine."

"Yes, certainly, grandfather," the fox responded. "The fish haven't much to eat these days. Dangle your tail down in the water and they will surely hang on. But you would have to sit patiently a long time. Could you do that?"

"Don't talk nonsense," the bear snarled. "Of course I could."

"Remember you will spoil everything if you are in a hurry," the fox said as the bear shambled away toward the glen of the elves.

Bruin found a hole in the ice and thrust his tail deep in the chilly water. The weather was cold, and ice was forming rapidly. The sun set and it grew dark, and the bear said to himself: "I have had enough of this sort of thing. Fish or no fish, I am going home."

But to his dismay he found that the hole in the ice had frozen over, and that his tail was held as if in a vise. To add to his alarm the elves just then discovered him and began shouting to each other: "Here is a bear in our glen! Drive him away! Drive him away!"

Instantly he had swarms of the little people all about him and each one was armed with a tiny bow and arrows and a spear hardly big enough for a baby. Their arrows and spears, though small, could sting, as the bear well knew from past experience, and in his fright he gave a mighty tug that broke his tail short off. Then away he scampered out of the glen as fast as he could go. His fine bushy tail was gone, and ever since that time all the bears have had short, stumpy tails.

The bear wanted to punish the fox, and he went in search of him. Reynard understood perfectly what he must expect, and he said to himself, "Unless I keep out of that fellow's way I shall lose something more than my tail."

Then he began speaking to his feet and other parts of himself. He would ask a question and pretend that the part addressed answered, though of course it was he who did all the talking. The conversation was like this:

"What would you do, my feet, if the bear was seeking my life?"

"We would run so fast that he could not catch you."

"What would you do, my ears, if the bear was seeking my life?"

"We would listen so keenly that we should hear all his plans."

"What would you do, my nose, if the bear was seeking my life?"

"I would smell so sharply that I could warn you of his coming while he was still afar off."

"What would you do, my tail, if the bear was seeking my life?"

"I would steer you so straight that you would soon get beyond his reach."

Then the fox listened intently and sniffed the air suspiciously. "I must be off—danger is near," he said.

So he ran and ran until he left the mountains with their ice and snow behind. At last he came to a man mending a boat beside a river.

"Lend me your boat that I may cross over to the other side," the fox requested.

"Don't bother me," the man said gruffly. "I'm busy."

"But I need your boat to cross over this river," the fox said as he sat on his hind legs and looked up into the man's face.

"Stop your silly chatter!" the man ordered. "Stop it, or I will give you a bath in the water!"

"Oh, I wish I had a boat, I wish I had a boat!" the fox cried.

Then the man jumped up, seized the fox by the tail, and threw him far out into the stream. It happened that there was a little island near where the fox fell, and he scrambled out on that. After shaking the water from his fur, he sat down, and called, "Hasten, hasten, O fishes, and carry me to the other side!"

Immediately the fishes left the pools where they had been lurking and hurried to see who could get to the island first.

"I have won," the pike shouted. Then he said to the fox, "Jump on my back and I will carry you to the other shore."

"No, I thank you," the fox responded. "Your back is too weak. I should break it."

The eel wriggled to the front and said, "Try mine."

"You are too slippery," the fox objected. "I would slide off and be drowned."

"You won't slide off my back," the perch said, coming forward.

"Good gracious, no!" the fox exclaimed, "not while you have such a spiny fin right in the middle of it; but I would be very uncomfortable."

At this moment a fine salmon swam up and said, "Well, you can have no fault to find with me."

"You are the person I want," the fox said. "Come close to the shore so I can get on your back without wetting my feet." The salmon swam as near the island as he could, and the fox stepped carefully on his back and was carried swiftly to the opposite bank. I think the fox must still be on that side of the river, for I have never heard of his returning.